VIOLET REVERIE

Violet Reverie by Talbot Finch
Published by Talbot Finch

talbotfinch.com

Cover by Luisa Galstyan

ISBN: 979-8-9861933-0-4

1

December 1883

The cold night air whipped outside Nathan's stately bedroom window. With the curtains drawn back, he watched flecks of snow whirl by on the wind. Only a week into December, it was unseasonably early for snow, more especially so here at the summer home. He pulled his robes around himself tightly. Keeping warm was a losing fight, and he hated the winter months for it. The cold was already beginning to settle into his bones.

The candlelight of the bedroom flickered in his periphery. Shadows danced on the walls around him, and from the corner of his eye, Nathan could see that their movements were not in sync with the rhythm of the candles. They moved on their own accord and, in momentary flashes, appeared to take the shape of people standing in the room with him. But he paid them no attention. Outside, a small cluster of snowflakes swirled in front of the window for just a moment too long, suspended in midair, as if slowing themselves to peer in at him before they continued on their way.

There was a hum in the air tonight, a vibration that filled Nathan's senses. He tried to ignore it, as he did with many things in life, but it wasn't easy. All throughout the house there was a quiet symphony playing only for those who knew how to listen—creaking boards and popping joints and groaning supports.

He heard the floorboards whisper to the walls, relaying a conversation from elsewhere in the house:

The Estate Manager confessed to the Housekeeper that he can no longer care for the grounds at his old age.

They need a groundskeeper, someone new, to help during spring.

Nathan sighed and drew the curtains. His father—Viscount Hambleton—sent him away from their London home to live here nearly two months ago, but he still felt as though he were only vacationing, just as he had every summer as a boy with his family. Of course, his family wasn't with him now, and he wouldn't be returning to the city until he was welcomed back.

It was strange seeing the house during this time of year. Christmas was two weeks away, and the staff had begun decorating with greenery and ribbon. Nathan imagined that this was the first time in many decades this house had seen decorations like these. It was usually vacant during the holidays save for the staff that maintained the estate year 'round.

This would be his first Christmas apart from his family. Even when attending university, he'd always gone home for the winter holiday. It pained him a bit to imagine Christmas morning without his mother. Her unaffected enthusiasm for the holiday had always been infectious, and without her company, he could hardly muster any excitement at all. He had hoped that she would come to visit—without his father—but she mentioned nothing of the sort in her last letter.

After blowing out the last candle in the room, Nathan settled into bed. In the dark, he thought about his mother's letters, how grateful he was for them. They were a light in the winter darkness. It terrified him to think what he might do if they one day stopped arriving.

The house was like a vast, empty cave on Christmas Day. Every minuscule sound reverberated through the halls unceasingly, unperceived by everyone but Nathan. It had given him a terrible migraine. He felt as though a large thumbscrew had been placed around his temples and gradually tightened. The endless, looping echoes throughout the home built on each other, pulling at the threads of his already frayed nerves.

He spent most of the day in his bed and refused both breakfast and lunch. He knew, however, that his lack of appetite made the staff nervous—not only for his health but also for any consequences that could arise if Nathan's mother or father discovered that he hadn't eaten on Christmas. It may reflect poorly on the cook and kitchen staff.

Mrs. Fairchild, the summer home's housekeeper, had been in several times to check to see if he needed anything. He could tell that she was growing increasingly concerned about his state, and in the afternoon, among the incessant echoing, he heard a whisper carried from somewhere far away within the house:

"Perhaps we should send a telegram to Lord Hambleton. His mother will certainly want to know if he is ill."

Despite his aching head, Nathan decided to dress and make an appearance at dinner. Contending with his migraine was preferable to having his father become involved.

"Master Nathan," Mrs. Fairchild said in surprise when he entered the sitting room. "Are you feeling well, sir?"

Her concern put him at ease. He had always liked Mrs. Fairchild. She was a remarkably sensible and decisive woman, tending to the matters of the estate with deft efficiency and a bright disposition. Now, her keen brown eyes watched him worriedly as rogue strands of copper-red hair, having escaped the tidy knot she always wore, danced around her freckled face.

"I am. Thank you." If she noticed the tension in his voice, she didn't say anything. Not that she would. *'Servants should never offer any opinion to their employers, not even to say good morning or good night except in reply to salutation.'* House rules. His father's rules, rather.

Nathan could remember being a boy of four or five in their London home, watching his father from around a corner as he towered over a recently hired footman and berated him for wishing him a good morning without him saying so first. The young man's employment was subsequently ended.

"Will you be dining tonight, sir?" she asked.

"I will, yes. I'm glad to report that my appetite has returned with a vengeance," he lied through a smile.

"The cook will be pleased to hear it."

She turned to leave the room but before she could, Nathan spoke. "Um, Mrs. Fairchild?"

"Sir?"

"Will you join me? For dinner, I mean. I understand that it isn't customary for you to dine with me, but it is Christmas after all, and I—" He fidgeted with a cuff link. "I'd prefer not to eat alone on Christmas."

For the first time in his many years of knowing her, Mrs. Fairchild looked unsure of herself. "Sir, while I'm honored that you'd ask me to join you, I feel I must object on behalf of Lord Hambleton. He wouldn't approve of such informality."

Nathan's composure faltered. He pulled at his fingers and took a step toward her. "No, I know, and you certainly don't have to. But I'm not asking as your employer's son. Rather, as one soul to another. Please dine with me." He couldn't bear to be alone with the unrelenting susurrus any longer.

Though she was unaware of the whispers that plagued him, Nathan's eyes revealed his quiet desperation to her. She regarded him sympathetically. "Master Nathan, if it's what you wish, I shall dine with you."

He relaxed his shoulders and smiled honestly for the first time all day. "Thank you. Really, thank you."

"I'll ensure that the table is set appropriately. Excuse me, sir." With a sweeping tug on her dress, she turned and left him to his thoughts. The echoes were quieter.

2

Dinner with Mrs. Fairchild had saved Nathan's Christmas and his sanity. Their conversation had never been completely informal, but Nathan felt it was as close to talking with a friend as he had felt in a long while. He even convinced her to address him without a title. It was his opinion that titles should not exist between friends, regardless of social standing. She agreed under certain conditions, namely that she would only do so in private company. It did not set a good example for the rest of the staff to see her speaking with him casually. Further, when his family was visiting, she would never address him as anything less than "Master Nathan."

To his delight, Mrs. Fairchild told him that he may call her Jude so long that he also did so exclusively in private. The shift in their relationship from professionals to friends was slow at first. On more than a few occasions, Jude called him Master Nathan out of habit and had to remind herself that she was free to share her opinions with him. But after a few weeks' time, she warmed up, and they began talking plainly about the goings on around the estate. Occasionally, she would let slip some gossip about other members of the staff. He never told her that he had already heard most of the information as disembodied whispers floating through the house.

Living at the summer home had become more bearable with Jude to talk to, but Nathan still found himself lonely at times. He couldn't discuss everything with her—not the voices he heard or visions he saw or even the true reason he was sent away from London—which was, of course, the greater issue. There wasn't a soul on this earth that he could talk to about everything. He considered prayer as a means to relieve the burden of his secrets, but Nathan wasn't sure that he believed in God. Or at least, not the one he was raised to. He knew there was *something*. Some kind of force responsible for the things that plagued him. But it was not a comforting thought.

Along with his newfound friendship with Jude, he also had his mother's letters to keep him tethered to reality. In her most recent one, she told him about the guests they had to their manor on New Year's Day and that his older brother Daniel had begun courting a new woman. Sometimes, reading her letters, Nathan envied his family for being able to carry on with their lives as normal. The simplest of life's joys—socializing, courting—had always felt out of reach for him, and they seemed even farther away now. But still, he held no resentment against them. In fact, he very much looked forward to his mother's correspondence. They were his only connection to the world outside of the summer home.

Sometimes her letters were nostalgic, reminiscing on stories from Nathan's childhood; sometimes she spoke about the latest news circulating around the city. Nathan never knew exactly what would be in the next letter, but he knew with certainty what wouldn't be—she never once spoke of his father.

He tried to make his responses to her interesting, but there wasn't much to report. He spent most days reading novels by Dickens and poetry by Whitman and Housman. At least twice a week, he would practice violin. It was the same as he had always done, really, and it didn't make for an engaging letter.

Things weren't always mundane; though, he knew better than to write about them. One day in January, Nathan was reading in the conservatory—a room that protruded off the back of the house with large, wall-to-wall windows that overlooked the grounds. Outside, the wind rustled the dead leaves and twigs in the garden, and for a brief moment, the rustling sound took shape and became a melody, a delicate tune that sounded familiar to him. He stopped reading and tried to recall where he knew it, but it was just out of reach. So, he retrieved his violin to aid him.

Nathan had been practicing violin since he was a young boy, and it had become a skill in which he felt exceptionally competent. However, after a disturbing incident involving a performance he'd given to a small group of family friends when he was fourteen years old, he started playing exclusively in private. It was during this incident in which he made the alarming discovery that the pieces he diligently practiced and memorized would change as he played, mid-performance, without his realizing it. What's more, this unconscious improvisation that poured from him seemed to have an unpredictable emotional effect on those who listened. As such, when he wanted to practice now, he would move to the uppermost part of the house to be away from everyone. The staff, not knowing the true reason why, simply understood that he was not to be bothered while he played.

Today, however, something in Nathan felt uninhibited. Instead of hiding away in the attic, he simply returned to the conservatory and began to play. He cautiously began working out the notes to the tune he'd heard before. As he played, the melody became sharper in his mind, and he performed with greater confidence. Despite this, he still couldn't place where he'd heard it before. The more he played, the more he wondered if he really knew this song at all, or if it belonged to someone else's memories. There was a strange knowing he felt in the tips of his fingers as they slid along the fingerboard that this song had come to him from someplace far away, desperate to be heard.

In that moment, he felt eyes on him. He quickly lowered his instrument and turned around to see Jude standing in the doorway of the conservatory looking at him with a stunned look, tears welling in her eyes.

"How do you know that song?" she asked in a whisper.

Nathan was at a loss for words.

"My mother," Jude continued. "She used to sing it to us all the time when we were girls. She said it was a tune that her own mother created herself. I haven't heard it since—" She paused and pressed a hand to her mouth. "You may not remember this, you were very young, but I left the estate for a short time nearly twenty years ago."

Nathan finally found his words, "Yes, I remember there were a few summers when I was a boy that you weren't here. I remember because Daniel fancied you and he complained."

Jude let herself laugh at that. "Do you remember why I left?"

"No, I'm afraid I don't."

"I'd married." She sounded very tired then. "His name was John. He was my childhood sweetheart. We'd lost touch for several years, but he found me, and we fell in love." The welling tears finally spilled down over her cheeks. "Then he became ill. It started small. Just pain in his stomach, but it spread. And he— He just couldn't— We were still only newly-weds."

She crumpled to the floor, sobbing, and Nathan quickly kneeled beside her. He wasn't sure what to do, but he placed a steady hand on her back and hoped that she could tell how sorry he was, how much he wished he could do something for her.

They sat there in silence for several minutes as her cries gradually quieted. Nathan handed her a handkerchief from his pocket.

"I'm sorry," she said, wiping her eyes.

"Please don't apologize."

She gave him a weak smile. "That song… My mother was with me when John passed. I was hysterical. But, my mother, she held me as I cried. And she sang her mother's song for me again. I haven't heard it since that night."

Jude turned to look Nathan in the face, a question in her eyes. "How do you know it?" she asked in a small voice. At that moment, it seemed that she was ready to believe anything he told her.

For a second, Nathan considered lying, offering any explanation that would make him seem less strange and abnormal. But looking at Jude and the openness on her face, he opted for the truth instead. “I don’t know.”

She searched his eyes, debating whether to ask him more. But she seemed to think better of it and turned away. “Today is our anniversary,” she said.

A shiver went down Nathan’s spine, and he wouldn’t allow himself to consider the implications of how the song had found him on this day. The “how” wasn’t important, he thought. Only the outcome mattered, and for Jude that was catharsis. He took her hand and gave it a small squeeze. Without another word between them, he helped her to her feet.

3

"Your birthday is coming up, isn't it? Just a few weeks out now?" Jude was pouring afternoon tea for herself and Nathan in the sitting room.

He eyed her from over the top of his book. "It is, yes. The 25th. Why do you ask?"

"Well," she continued, adding sugar and cream to Nathan's tea the way he liked. "Would you like me to send out invitations to any friends? Perhaps, some of your classmates from university?"

He pretended to return to his book. "No, thank you. February is a dreadful month for travel. And besides that, I'm not fond of birthdays." He tried to sound light, but it was clear that Jude saw through him. She wasn't going to leave the subject.

"Regardless of February, you haven't had any visitors since you've arrived, you know. I'm sure it would be fine if you did. I'd be surprised if your parents expected you to live here without ever seeing your friends."

"You're my friend," he said, still pretending to read.

She gave him a patient look. "You're mine, too. But you're still a young man, after all. Now's the time to surround yourself with your mates and have parties, make memories. You're turning twenty-six for pity's sake."

Nathan stayed silent. In truth, he longed desperately for companionship, but he didn't have a choice in the matter.

Jude placed his tea on the side table next to his chair and took her seat across from him. She sipped on her tea quietly and decided not to press the matter any further.

He sighed. "Look, thank you. I do appreciate what you're saying. But I've never attracted friendships easily, and I've always struggled to maintain the few I've made."

Jude let some silence pass before she carefully spoke. "I remember even as a child you were always a bit… peculiar." She took another sip of her tea and continued, treading lightly, "I'm not sure if it's a gift or an affliction. I imagine it feels like both at times. And I also imagine it makes some people wary."

"Are you wary?"

She seemed to think on this for a moment. "No. I don't understand it completely, and sometimes it worries me that you don't seem to understand it completely either, but I trust your intentions."

He finally put his book down and properly looked at her. She smiled at him, and he found himself smiling back.

"Well," she said in a decided manner. "Small affair or not, we will need to do *something* to make your birthday memorable."

There'd been awful weather on the days leading up to his birthday, but still Jude and the rest of the staff were in good humor as they bustled around in preparation. Nathan had ultimately opted for a private celebration and kept the invite list exclusive to the house staff, ensuring it would be a modest event. Being the family's summer home, the estate and staff were smaller compared to most.

Nathan was fond of all of them and had grown to view them as a kind of surrogate family over the past few months. His birthday was the perfect excuse to give them all the night off—a small gesture of gratitude. Unfortunately, it meant that they had to work diligently the day before the party to make up for the time they would spend celebrating. Of course, too, there was a lot that needed to be done by the kitchen staff on the day of, but Nathan had insisted that they keep the dishes simple. He also insisted that they take shifts amongst themselves so that they all had an opportunity to leave the kitchen and join the festivities.

"You run a rather unconventional ship, you know," Jude teased him. "But we all appreciate it."

"Well, I appreciate all of you. It's the least I could do."

———

Nathan woke up on the day of his birthday with a strange feeling in his right hand. It was buzzing as though there was a swarm of bees beneath his skin. He did his best to ignore it and readied himself for the day ahead.

He examined himself in the mirror at the washstand; it stood in the corner of his room near the window, and he could see himself clearly in the morning light. Being midwinter, his thin face seemed especially pale. He tousled his short, mousy brown hair, then dragged his hands down the sides of his face, stopping to scratch the stubble that grew in uneven patches along his jaw.

Since leaving London months ago, Nathan had to start dressing and shaving himself as he no longer had a valet. He supposed that he could have instructed the summer home's footman to fill in but being dressed and groomed by someone else had always felt invasive to him. And now especially, he did not want anyone to see his shoulders and back… The scabs had healed since October, but unsightly marks still remained. He was ashamed to be seen as he was.

After shaving, as he splashed water on his face to remove the excess cream, he looked down into the washstand's ornate porcelain basin and saw a change. The bowl was normally decorated with elaborate blue flowers and foliage, but instead of this, he now saw a scene of a kite flying amongst storm clouds, tethered to the earth by its string which was fastened securely around a large, sturdy boulder. He stared at it for a moment before scooping more water into his hands and giving his face a final rinse. After drying himself, he looked back into the basin and saw flowers there once again.

The day carried on more or less exactly how Nathan imagined it would. Everyone convened for a light, leisurely lunch and then retired to the drawing room. They played several rounds of Charades and Lookabout. After that, Emily, one of the maids, suggested Reverend Crawley's Game which turned out to be a riot. To begin the game, everyone stood together and held hands in a complicated pattern so that they became a giant knot of intertwining arms. Then, they had to work out how to untangle themselves without letting go of anyone's hand. With everyone twisting and contorting in absurd and awkward ways, there was a nonstop string of giggles ringing through the air. Jude had an unmistakable and contagious laugh that carried over the group and infected the others.

By the time everyone had gotten untangled, Nathan was flushed and lightheaded with laughter. He couldn't remember the last time he'd felt so giddy.

Next, William, the footman, suggested a song. Someone asked Nathan if he would play for them on his violin. He lied and said that his bow needed to be rehaired but agreed to play for them on the piano. He wasn't as competent a pianist as a violinist, and perhaps even less so now with the tingling sensation in his hand, but he could play well enough for the simpler singalongs being requested.

Then, it was time for dinner. Per Nathan's request, the food was simple, but it was no less delicious. There were lively discussions and stories all around the table as everyone had their fill of food and sherry.

Jude leaned over to Nathan. "This was a splendid idea. The house needed this, a bit of joy. Winter can be hard on morale, you know."

He grinned. All throughout the afternoon, he'd felt electricity crackling in the air from everyone's bright spirits. "You're right, this was a splendid idea. Thank you for insisting that I celebrate my birthday."

She laughed and took another sip of sherry. On Nathan's other side, old Mr. Millican, the estate manager, stood from the table and excused himself.

"Master Nathan, forgive me, but I must attend to a few matters."

"Can't it wait until tomorrow, Mr. Millican? You'd be sorely missed here."

Jude chimed in suddenly. "Master Nathan, I beg your pardon, but that's my mistake. I meant to inform you earlier, but I'm afraid I forgot. We have a new groundskeeper coming to the estate to help with the coming spring."

"It's looking like we'll be having an early one this year, sir," Mr. Millican added.

"He was supposed to arrive several days ago," Jude continued. "But the poor weather made the roads impassable by carriage. I'm sorry, I should've told you sooner, sir. I know this isn't an ideal time."

"Mrs. Fairchild, please, there is no need to apologize. I couldn't think of a better time for him to join us. When will he be arriving, Mr. Millican?"

"It should be within the hour, sir."

"Well, once he's had a chance to put away his things, please tell our new groundskeeper that he's welcome to join our party if he would like."

After dinner in the drawing room, someone suggested they play Blindman's Buff. Mrs. Blake, the cook, went first. They placed a blindfold over her eyes, spun her around in circles a few times, and then scattered as she tried to grab someone. She managed to catch Jude, and her laugh gave her away immediately.

Then, it was Jude's turn to stumble around wearing the blindfold. She'd touched one of the kitchen staff first, but she guessed wrong and had to try again. Next, she managed to catch Emily and guessed right.

The game continued until it was finally Nathan's turn. He was especially good at games like this. People didn't realize how much their footsteps and rustling clothes said about them. In fact, as a child, he was so good at this game that he was often accused of cheating. For this reason, Nathan purposefully guessed wrong when he caught William first.

He resumed moving around in the dark with his arms cautiously outstretched, giggles and whispers coming from all directions. Every now and then someone far away from him would call out *"Over here, blind man!"*

With a broad, searching swipe of his arm, the buzzing in his right hand surged momentarily as if it had reacted to something near him. Impulsively, Nathan waved his hand over the same area, found the spot where the sensation surged again, and pressed forward, following it.

In a short distance, the feeling in his hand had spread down his arm and became almost unbearable. It had grown rapidly from a slight tingling to a searing, unstoppable humming that was so overwhelming it made Nathan's ears ring. Then, just as the noise grew so loud that he could hear nothing else, it stopped in an instant as his hand came into contact with something solid.

The sensation in his hand had gone, too, as if it had never existed in the first place. Everything was now quiet and still.

As if afraid the thing he touched would disappear, Nathan scrambled to pull the blindfold off his face. He saw before him what his hand had drawn him to—a man, just shorter than Nathan, who looked to be about his age. The man had a sturdy build, square jaw, and short waves of black hair with full brows and lashes to match. The contrast of his pale skin and dark hair created an understated drama about him that was punctuated by humble, blue eyes.

He wasn't sure how long he'd been staring, but it seemed like no time had passed for those around him because all at once Nathan heard their outcries:

"Oi! You can't take off your blindfold!"

"That's cheating, that is!"

"No peeking, you know!"

Nathan was quick to compose himself. "I know, I know. You're right, it is cheating," he said good-naturedly. "But, in all fairness, how on earth was I supposed to guess who this was?"

They all laughed, including the stranger standing in the doorway who Nathan had just touched.

"I'm sorry, sir," the man began. He glanced around the room with a sheepish grin, his ears and cheeks had gone a slight shade of red from everyone's attention. "I didn't mean to disrupt your game. I was told there was a celebration going on."

Mr. Millican stepped from around him and dutifully announced, "Mr. Watts, may I introduce you to the Honorable Nathaniel Hambleton. Master Nathan, this is our new groundskeeper, Mr. Peter Watts."

Nathan extended a hand. It didn't react this time when it got nearer to him. Peter took it and smiled.

"It's wonderful to meet you, sir."

"The same to you, Mr. Watts."

4

My Dear Mother,

Thank you for your last letter and your birthday wishes. I had the strangest encounter on the night of my birthday; I met a man under rather unconventional circumstances. My guests and I were playing a parlor game in which I was blindfolded (Yes, it was the Blindman's game you dislike). As luck would have it, my hand guided me directly to the one stranger among them. It was, of course, impossible for me to guess the name of someone I'd never met! We all found the situation rather amusing. However, I almost can't believe it was a coincidence. It felt more like serendipity—like my body was compelled by something beyond its will.

The stranger turned out to be the summer home's new groundskeeper. He seems like a kind and humble man; he got along very well with the others, too. I think he will do a splendid job here on the estate. However, I keep thinking about the peculiar nature in which we met. It strikes me as the beginning of a comedy play or something of the sort. I find myself wondering what may be in store as this tale unfolds.

Forgive my musings. I know that I'm being fanciful. You always said I possessed an imagination that rivaled that of Lewis Carroll. Anyway, I hope you and the others are well. I look forward to your next letter.

Your Fanciful Son,

Nathaniel

The early March sunlight flooded the study and spilled onto Nathan's writing desk. He sat in silence, watching the glittering particles of dust pass through the sunbeam. It was still quite cold, but it was beginning to look less like winter. The sun gradually positioned itself higher in the sky with each passing week, a signal to the world below that spring was on its way.

Nathan allowed himself to watch the ray of sunshine for a moment longer. Something in him relaxed thinking about the end of winter. Since arriving at the summer home in late October, he had barely left the house. At first, he'd been too depressed to leave his bed. Then, by the time he could muster the energy to dress himself in the mornings, the biting cold had set in and kept him indoors. For months now, he's longed to be outside, to feel the warmth of the sun, to lose himself in a book by the lake. And now, after a winter that seemed like it would never end, the subtle first signs of spring were finally evident and with them came a renewed sense of optimism.

He turned back to the letter he'd just finished and read it over. It'd been nearly two weeks since his birthday party, and in that time, Nathan had found himself thinking frequently about his introduction to the new groundskeeper. It wasn't often that he tried to understand the strange happenings and sensations he experienced. In fact, he'd made it a point to avoid thinking about them at all for fear that giving them unnecessary attention would exacerbate the issue. However, something about this encounter had piqued his interest.

Peter had seemed to be adjusting well to life on the estate. He took to his work quickly and with enthusiasm. As the groundskeeper, he spent most of his time outside of the main house, so opportunities for impromptu conversation were few. Nathan had been tempted on more than one occasion to seek him out and ask him questions directly, though to what end he wasn't sure. So instead, he tried to put thoughts of Peter out of his mind entirely. That was, until he woke up a few days later and found that the questions he'd tried to suppress had grown loud enough to manifest into incessant whispering.

Who is he? Why am I drawn to him? Did he feel the hum, too, that night?

These questions repeated themselves again and again, their sound layering and building on each other. By late morning, Nathan couldn't sit still and had walked every inch of the house trying to get away from the whispering, but it followed him.

A blanket of rain clouds had moved in the night before and covered everything as far as one could see. It made him feel even more agitated and trapped. He tried to think back to the calm, sunny morning he spent at his writing desk just a few days before, but the droning of voices made it impossible. The questions grew louder and more insistent, until it sounded as if the home was filled, from wall to wall, with loud, chattering bodies.

Finally, unable to bear it anymore, Nathan all but fled the house. He hadn't even bothered to put on a jacket before walking out into the rain. Normally one to curse the cold, he welcomed it now. The rain, light but steady, cooled the smoldering tension that had been building in his face.

He stood there, a few short yards from the house, watching the smoke of his breath slowly become steadier. The rain was the only sound he heard; his thoughts were quiet, at last. While it was an utter relief, he was certain it was conditional. The voices, he knew, carried on with their murmuring and muttering inside the house, awaiting his return. He also knew what might stop them.

Taking one more deep breath of cool air, he turned and followed the walkway around to the back of the home. The trees surrounding the property, still bare and sleeping, stood like spindly, silhouetted hands reaching toward the overcast sky. Despite its steadfast pattering, the rain made the world feel especially quiet now—a small blessing to Nathan.

He focused on the yellow light coming from the windows of the barn. The "barn" was actually a small group of buildings that had been designed and built together—stable, carriage house, and shed. On the land to the left of the barn stood the greenhouse. From the walkway, Nathan could just make out a shadow moving behind the glass walls, lit by the soft glow of an oil lantern. He made his way to the door.

Upon entering, Peter, who had been hunched over several pots of long-dead plants, looked over his shoulder. When he noticed who was there, he swiftly straightened up.

"Master Nathan?"

It had only just occurred to Nathan how he must have looked. His hair was damp from the rain, the shoulders of his shirt were soaked through, and his cheeks were bright and flushed from the cold. He awkwardly cleared his throat.

"Mr. Watts, how great to see you. I wanted to pay you a visit and ask how you were getting along here at the estate."

With uncertainty, Peter looked over Nathan from head to toe. Brows drawn together, he looked like he wanted to ask something, but simply answered the question instead. "I'm getting along very well, sir. Thank you. It's a lovely property."

"It is, yes. I've always enjoyed being here. This home has belonged to my family for generations," he told him. "Are you from this part of England?"

"No, sir. In fact, it's my first time being this far south."

"Oh? How did you hear that we were in need of a groundskeeper?"

"I heard about the opening in London—"

"So, you're from London, then? Whereabouts? And, where in the city did you learn gardening?"

Peter tried to keep a neutral expression but couldn't completely hide his amusement. "Will there be a written portion to this examination as well, sir?"

It took Nathan a moment to realize he was being teased. Staff never made jokes in the presence of their employers and certainly none at their expense. It would've gone over very poorly with his father, but to Nathan it was refreshing, despite his embarrassment.

"You'll have to excuse me," he said, dropping his head with a sheepish smile. "New faces have been something of a rarity around here lately. I'm afraid my excitement has made me forget my manners."

Peter gave a lopsided smile. "It's quite all right, sir. As for London, I'm not from there either. I grew up on a farm in a small village a few hours north of London by horse. When I heard about the groundskeeper position, I was working as an apprentice for a master gardener in the city and living with family friends."

"Ah, I see," Nathan said. "Well, thank you for indulging my curiosity. I've bothered you quite enough for one day, I think." He gave a nod and turned to leave.

"Sir," Peter began, stopping him. "Mr. Millican said that he would ask you what sorts of things you'd like to see grown here," he gestured around him to the greenhouse, "but, I suppose if you're here now, I could just as well ask you myself."

"Oh, um," Nathan said, looking helplessly around the space. He supposed that he should have opinions on things like this, but botany and gardening were not his forte. "I, uh, trust your judgment and expertise on the matter." He waved his hand vaguely. "A variety of flowers and fruits, I suppose. Um, I'm partial to strawberries—"

Just then, in his mind's eye, Nathan saw the greenhouse fill with hundreds of small plants with brilliant purple flowers. As they grew and bloomed before him, he could smell their soft and sweet scent. From Mr. Watts's breast pocket, a small cluster of the flowers sprouted up and adorned his coat like a boutonniere. Then, just as quickly as the image came to him, it was gone again, and the greenhouse was once more occupied only with withered and dried things.

From the pattering of the rain on the glass roof, a word caught Nathan's ear. "Violet," he said.

Peter looked at him with surprised, injured eyes. "I'm sorry?"

Nathan had apparently touched on something sensitive and hastily tried to recover. "Violets," he continued as lightly as he could. "You may grow whatever else you would like, but I want there to be violets. Strawberries and violets. That's my only request."

"Oh." Peter visibly relaxed, though he still seemed uneasy. "Right, of course, sir."

The rain grew louder above them, and it was then that Nathan realized how cold and wet he was. A shiver overtook him.

"Perhaps, I should get you back indoors, sir," said Peter, looking Nathan over again, from his soaked hair to his lack of appropriate attire. "I imagine you may need an umbrella. There's one in the barn, I think. I'll fetch it for you." With that, he grabbed his hat from a nearby wrought iron table and pulled his coat tighter around him. The groundskeeper left the greenhouse, and Nathan watched through the rain-coated glass as he hurriedly made for the barn.

Alone, Nathan thought back to his vision of violets and reflected on Peter's reaction. He wanted to probe further but decided that he'd asked enough questions for one day.

When Peter returned with an umbrella, Nathan began to thank him and reach out for it, but the groundskeeper interrupted.

"I can walk you to the house, sir. It isn't any trouble."

Nathan considered his seemingly abrupt and strange visit to the greenhouse, soaked through with rain and armed with personal questions. Not a great impression, he thought. He must've seemed unwell, or worse, unstable.

Peter probably didn't trust him to find his own way back to the house. Nathan thought it wise not to protest.

"That's very kind. Thank you."

As they walked, Peter kept a guiding arm around Nathan's shoulders. It could have easily seemed patronizing, but it felt instead like a friendly gesture, as if they had known each other for many years. The word *informal* came to Nathan's mind in his father's voice, but he quickly replaced it with another word in his own. *Sincere.* He smiled to himself.

"I beg your pardon, Mr. Watts, but is this your first time working at a manor?"

Peter stopped and faced him with a nervous look. "I'm sorry, sir. Have I done something wrong?"

"No, not wrong. There are just small things I've observed. You seem less…rigid than most other staff members."

"Oh," he said, uncertainly. "Well, sir, to answer your question—Yes, this is my first time working at a manor. Is it obvious?"

"A bit," Nathan admitted. "If I may be so bold, with whom did you interview?"

"Mr. Audrey, sir."

Mr. Audrey was the longtime butler for the Hambleton family's London home. He was a shrewd judge of character and therefore permitted to conduct interviews for lesser staff positions. Additionally, he knew precisely how his employer, Lord Hambleton, liked his estates to be managed. Having known him for years, Nathan was surprised to hear that Peter had received Mr. Audrey's approval.

"Mr. Davies, the gardener I'd been apprenticing for, put in a good word for me," he confessed. "He's friends with Mr. Audrey. That was how I'd heard of the opening in the first place."

"I see. So, it was favoritism that brought you here," Nathan said with a wry smirk.

Peter was too anxious to recognize he was being chaffed. "I am very sorry, Master Nathan," he said earnestly, then paused. "Do you feel that I'm unfit to work here, sir?"

"Not at all," he reassured. "On the whole, I'd say you seem to be getting along quite well."

Peter relaxed. "Thank you, sir."

"A word of warning, though," Nathan continued, lowering his voice, "My father will be harder to please. For him, performance is not judged solely on skill or productivity. You see, he's an unbearable stickler for etiquette. You needn't worry yourself now, though. He will not likely make an appearance here until the summer months."

"Thank you for your candor, Master Nathan. And I do apologize for any lack of professionalism on my part. You can be assured, it won't be a problem again, sir."

"Well, for your sake, I trust you will be on your best behavior whenever my father visits. However, I am not like my father, so when I am acting as the head of this estate," Nathan smiled, "I hope that you continue as you were. In fact, when we are alone, you must feel free to call me Nathan."

The groundskeeper positively beamed. "Thank you, sir! Er, I mean, Nathan. You can call me Peter, if you'd like."

"Peter," Nathan repeated. "It's a pleasure to make your casual acquaintance."

"The same to you," Peter said, grinning still. Then, he leaned in closer, conspiratorially, "Forgive my asking, but you said your father would be here in the summer. Don't families such as yours typically stay in the city during the summer months?"

"Ah, yes. The Season. You know, for as proper as my father strives to be, he has never cared for the social season. He's never said as much, but I don't think he cares for the sheer number of people and obligations. So, he endures the early months then brings us all here, usually in

July. In our circles, the "Hambleton Summer Holiday" has become something of an ongoing joke, which my father has never found very amusing. His excuse to others has always been that my mother is sensitive to the oppressive heat of London summers, and she dutifully plays along."

Peter grinned. "Well, I'll do what I can around here to have things ready for this year's Hambleton Summer Holiday."

Nathan smiled in kind. "I'm sure it'll be a memorable one."

"Personally, I'm quite ready for summer," Peter shivered. "Let's get you indoors." He put his sturdy arm back around Nathan's shoulder and continued to walk him to the house.

When they arrived, Jude met them in the foyer and immediately made a fuss over Nathan. "Master Nathan! You're wet, head to toe! My goodness. Let's get you into dry clothes and in front of the hearth." She rushed to his side and began leading him away. Before they left, she called out behind her, "Thank you, Peter."

"Yes, thank you," Nathan agreed and glanced back at him.

"You're very welcome, Master Nathan," he said dutifully and bowed in an exaggerated display of decorum. It earned him an amused grin.

As he was led to his chambers, Nathan took notice of the sound of his and Jude's footsteps. The house was quiet. The voices had stopped.

5

The following morning Nathan awoke with the beginnings of a cold. He cursed the damp weather and spent the day in bed.

"I was worried about this," Jude said when she'd found him shivering under his blanket. She placed a hand on his forehead and uttered a *tsk*. "You're running a fever, I'm afraid. Should I fetch the doctor?"

"Ah," Nathan waved a hand, "I'll be fine. It's just some congestion. I'll be back to my normal self in a day or two."

He received his meals in bed and did little more than read and sleep. Jude checked on him often and stoked the flames in the fireplace, ensuring his room stayed pleasantly warm. Nathan did get up once to walk around his chambers and stretch his legs, but it exhausted him after only a short distance.

Throughout the afternoon, in between moments of shallow sleep and groggy wakefulness, thoughts of Peter and their conversation from the day before came to him. He thought absently to himself that he would like to speak with him more when he was well again.

As the day pressed on, the soreness in his throat worsened, and by evening, he found swallowing exceedingly painful. After dinner, Mrs. Blake made him a hot toddy which did offer some relief for his throat. However, the congestion in his nose and behind his eyes had grown worse as well, and the pressure had built so much that Nathan found himself with a dreadful headache. The chances of getting a night of restful sleep were poor. Still, the whisky from the toddy had made him drowsy, and he was able to doze off despite his discomfort.

His rest was short-lived, though, for in the early hours of the morning, Nathan was awoken by overwhelming nausea. He only just managed to grab his chamber pot from beneath his bed before vomiting. He was sick several more times before his stomach finally settled. In the dark, he sat on the floor for some time, trying to catch his breath. The retching had worsened his headache. He leaned his head back against the bed and closed his eyes trying to will the pain away.

A timid knock came from the door.

"Yes," Nathan croaked.

The door opened to reveal a shy Emily in her nightgown holding a chamberstick. "Beg your pardon, Master Nathan, but I thought I heard you from my room. You sounded very ill. Are you all right, sir?"

"Emily," he said as brightly as he could. "Yes, I'm all right. Thank you. I'm feeling better now, but I would greatly appreciate some water."

"Yes, of course, sir," she said and hurriedly made for the kitchen.

The door to his chambers was left slightly ajar, and he watched as the candlelight in the hallway outside grew dimmer with the sound of Emily's fading footsteps. He sat staring blankly into the dark hall. The world swayed around him. His vision shifted in and out of focus. He thought for a moment that he might fall asleep before she returned.

Then, suddenly, he heard footsteps coming from the darkness outside his door. But they were not Emily's light, anxious steps. These were heavy and slow and not accompanied by candlelight. These were steps from someone moving through the house in utter darkness. They grew nearer, louder.

"Hello?" Nathan called out. "Who's there?"

There was no response. Only the ominous sound of someone slowly approaching. Nathan felt a chill in the air and an irrepressible feeling of dread. He clambered to his feet and found his way to the bedside table. He grabbed the matchbox from the drawer, and with trembling fingers, struggled to light the candle he kept close by. The footsteps were nearly there.

Finally, the wick caught the flame, and he spun with the candlestick in hand to face the door. The steps had stopped. Whatever had made them stood just outside.

"Who is it?" he yelped.

In response, the door opened slowly and squeaked on its hinges. Behind it stood a towering, shadowed figure. From the far end of the room, with only the light of his candle, Nathan could make out the vague details of a well-tailored suit adorning the figure in the doorway, but the face of the man remained obscured by darkness.

His mouth had gone dry, but he managed to bark out, "Show yourself!"

The figure stepped into the room.

In the kitchen, Emily had gotten both a glass of water for Master Nathan as well as a clean washcloth so that he could wipe his mouth of the sick. She grabbed her chamberstick and was beginning the walk back to his room when she heard a terrible scream that made her blood run cold. It had been Master Nathan, she was certain. She all but ran to his chambers, still holding onto the glass of water and paying little mind to the mess she made as she moved.

When she arrived at the threshold of Nathan's bedroom, she found him on the floor curled up on his side with his hands raised over his head as if trying to protect himself. On the carpet next to him, there was an extinguished candle on its side, lying in a small puddle of its own wax. Nathan was yelling in shrill, hysterical phrases at something that she could not see.

She looked around the room anxiously to see if someone was there with them, but it was completely empty. This unnerved her even more. The hairs on her neck stood on end.

"Master Nathan?" she asked, helplessly.

He didn't respond. He didn't even seem to know she was there.

It was then that several others came rushing in from the hall wearing their nightshirts, too. At the head of the group was Jude. She rushed past Emily and crouched down next to Nathan, despite his yelling and wild movements.

"Master Nathan," she said firmly and loudly. "Master Nathan, it's all right." She managed to place a steadying hand on one of his arms and wiped away strands of sweat-soaked hair from his forehead with her other. She then turned to Emily and beckoned her to bring the washcloth and the now half-empty glass of water. "Go fetch a basin and a pitcher of cool water. We'll need more than this," Jude said to her, taking the glass and cloth. "He's got a very high fever."

Emily nodded and scurried away through the small crowd of staff members that had gathered outside of the room. Jude dampened the cloth as best she could with the water she had and began gently wiping Nathan's face. He carried on with his shouts and indiscernible muttering for a bit longer, but eventually, he began to respond to her calm words and the cooling washcloth. Emily returned with the pitcher and basin, and with them, Jude wrung out the rag with fresh water and continued wiping his face.

"Everything's fine, see? You're fine," Jude gently reassured.

An awareness had finally returned to Nathan's eyes, and he warily looked around the room. He saw a cluster of familiar and concerned faces standing in his doorway, watching him intently. He glanced up at Jude whose eyes were filled with worry despite her apparent composure.

"Are you feeling better, sir?" she asked.

"I-I don't," he began, struggling to find his words. "I'm terribly sorry, everyone. I don't know what— I was just..."

“Sir, if I may, you’ve got a terrible fever,” she said, continuing to press the washcloth to his forehead. “I believe it was playing tricks on your senses. That’s all. There is no need to apologize.”

A murmur of agreement came from the others. Nathan looked at them again and this time caught sight of Peter standing among them toward the back of the group. Seeing him, Nathan was struck then with a pang of embarrassment and shame.

“Please, I’d like some privacy,” he said quietly to Jude. She nodded.

“Right, then,” she said to the others with a note of finality. “I think it’s best that we let Master Nathan alone. He needs to rest, and so do the lot of you.”

She ushered the crowd out and thanked Emily for her help before closing the door behind them. She turned then back to Nathan, who was still on the floor but sitting up now with his face buried in his hands.

“Are you all right?” she asked.

“Yes, I think I am now,” he mumbled. “But, what a commotion. I’m mortified. They must all think I’m a madman.”

“Oh, don’t be hard on yourself.” She helped him to his feet and back into bed. “Nothing about it was your fault. I’m not worried about your sanity in the slightest. I am, however, worried about this fever.” She put a hand to his forehead again and then to his cheek. “It’s better than it was, but it still isn’t good. I’ll send for the doctor first thing. Dawn will break in only a few hours.”

“Will you stay with me until then?” Even to his own ears, it sounded like a childish request, but he did not want to be alone. He was frightened. The man from the hallucination lingered in his mind, his presence still in the air.

“I’d fully intended to, whether you had wanted me here or not,” Jude disclosed to him. She lit one of the oil lamps in the room and blew out her chamberstick.

Nathan felt relieved both at the light and in knowing he wouldn't be alone. "Thank you, Jude."

"Of course," she said and pulled up a chair to his bedside. She grabbed the basin of water and set it on her lap. "I'll try to keep the fever down, but don't mind me. You try to get some rest."

Nathan didn't think he would be able to get back to sleep after all of the excitement he'd had, but in only a few short minutes, exhaustion overcame him, and he fell asleep with Jude at his side and a cool cloth on his brow.

6

At daybreak, Jude sent the stableman to retrieve the village doctor. Nathan was still in bed and had barely finished his first cup of tea when the doctor arrived and began his examination. He was a short, jolly man with plump, plum-like cheeks, a balding crown, and white whiskers. He never appeared to be without a smile, and he had a quality about him that Nathan could only describe as rural.

"Good heavens!" he said upon entering the room and first seeing Nathan. "You certainly are in a poor state, aren't you? I heard you gave everyone a proper fright last night. Bad fever, was it?" He placed his black leather medical bag onto the bed next to Nathan and began rummaging around inside. "I am Dr. Beverley. And I presume that you are Mr. Nathaniel Hambleton."

"Yes, doctor, that's right."

"Well, that is good, isn't it? Otherwise, I'd be in the wrong home," he said with a chuckle and produced a thermometer from his bag. He held it up to the light from the window for a moment and squinted through his round spectacles. "I'm surprised we haven't crossed paths sooner. I've been the doctor in this village for the better part of three decades now. Though, perhaps, it isn't so surprising. As I understand it, your family tends to visit only for a couple of months out of the year."

"That's right. During the summer."

Dr. Beverley gave the thermometer a small shake with his wrist and then placed it in Nathan's mouth. While they waited, he used his stethoscope to check Nathan's heart and lungs. Jude stood by the door, watching silently and wringing her hands.

"Well," said the doctor, examining the thermometer through squinted eyes again, "that fever you've got, Mr.

Hambleton, is not one I'd take lightly. Continue to use a damp cloth to keep it down."

"I certainly will," Nathan assured.

"Good man," the doctor said approvingly. "Your lungs seem healthy at the moment, and I'd very much like them to stay that way! Wouldn't you?"

He smiled despite himself. Dr. Beverley had an easy charm about him. "Yes, I suppose I would," he agreed.

"Very good! Then, I would like you to use a mustard plaster to combat the congestion."

Nathan groaned. He hated mustard plasters; they almost always made him blister. "Dr. Beverley, I don't mean to be a difficult patient, but I get terrible burns from plasters."

"Sensitive skin, eh? Well, that shouldn't be any trouble so long as you don't leave it on for too long. I'd say no longer than ten minutes at a time. Applied at least six times per day."

"Yes, doctor," he sighed.

"Excellent," Dr. Beverley beamed. "You'd also do well to consume plenty of warm beverages and soups." Nathan had already been doing this but agreed anyway. "Manage the fever and congestion like we discussed, and you should be in the pink again within a week, I'd say. All the same, I'll pay you another visit in a few days' time to see how you're getting on."

The doctor left, and Jude stayed with Nathan for the remainder of the morning, seeing to his fever. She also helped him with the plasters—mixing mustard powder with water into a paste and applying it to his chest. Per Dr. Beverley's instructions, leaving the plasters on for only ten minutes at a time kept the skin irritation to a minimum.

By lunch, both the fever and congestion had improved some. Jude took the opportunity to excuse herself to her own chambers and rest after the long night she'd had. Nathan rested, too.

After his fourth plaster of the day, Nathan was sitting in bed and reading when he heard a knock at his door. "Come in."

The door opened and Peter stepped in, fidgeting slightly. Surprised, Nathan sat up quickly and accidentally let his book fall shut without noting his page. Upon seeing Peter, Nathan had immediately broken out into a cold sweat and felt his cheeks burn with shame. He was there to give his resignation after the incident last night, Nathan thought. Anyone would be scared away after a spectacle like that.

"I hope I'm not bothering you," Peter said, taking a few cautious steps forward.

"No!" Nathan said hastily. "Certainly not. No bother at all."

Peter looked him over and gave a sympathetic look. "You're still looking a bit feverish, aren't you?"

This made Nathan's cheeks burn even more. "I couldn't say," he laughed awkwardly. "I've been avoiding my reflection. I feel so ghastly, I'm afraid I wouldn't recognize myself."

Peter smiled at this and sat down in the chair next to the bed that Jude had been in most of the morning. "I'm glad to see you haven't lost your sense of humor," he said. "You gave us all a right scare last night."

"Yes, I know, and I can't apologize enough," Nathan said sheepishly.

"Please, you don't need to. You just had us worried, is all. I wanted to pay you a visit to make sure you were all right. I asked Mrs. Fairchild if I could, and she said yes, but not to linger."

That sounded like her; Nathan smiled. The tension in his shoulders dissipated. "That's very thoughtful. I appreciate the visit," he said. "I worried that after last night's excitement people might feel inclined to leave."

Peter shrugged and simply said, "It'll take more than a cold to run me off."

"I'm relieved to hear it."

"Although, I must admit," Peter continued, "I'd only ever heard of people having fever hallucinations. I'd never seen it happen before."

"It's awful," Nathan told him. "Like having a nightmare but being awake for it. It used to happen a lot when I got sick as a child. I'd forgotten how bad it could be."

"That does sound awful," Peter winced. "I can't imagine what you must've seen last night. You looked utterly terrified. Just thinking about it sends a shiver down my spine."

Nathan shifted uncomfortably. For a moment, he considered telling Peter about the figure he'd seen, but he couldn't bring himself to recount the experience. Before he could think how to change the subject, Jude entered after a short, perfunctory knock.

"I'm sorry to interrupt, Master Nathan, but I need to give you another plaster. Peter, if you would be so kind as to give Master Nathan some privacy."

"Yes, of course." He jumped to his feet and gave Nathan a quick nod. "Feel better soon, sir," he said before hurrying out of the room.

Jude gave Nathan a curious look once he was gone. "He asked me if he could see you," she said as she began mixing the plaster. "I wasn't sure if I should let him, but he said he wanted to make sure you were feeling better after last night."

"That's right, he did," Nathan confirmed.

She hummed thoughtfully. "You know, I think that's rather sweet. Bit informal though."

Nathan laughed out loud then, much to Jude's surprise. "I had that very thought only two days ago and told him as much. Yes, he is a bit informal. I told him not to worry, though, so long as my father wasn't around."

"I see," she said with a knowing grin. "You two certainly became friends quickly, didn't you?"

"I wouldn't go so far as to say friends. Though, I would like to know him better. There's something about his character I find charming." He began unbuttoning the top of his nightshirt for the plaster. "Or it could simply be that I'm desperate for companionship."

Jude stopped spreading the paste onto his chest and gave him a sympathetic look. "There aren't many young men your age around here to talk to, are there? Although, I suppose that puts Peter in the same ship as you, doesn't it? Perhaps, with more time, you will become friends after all."

"Perhaps so."

"Right," she said, surveying her work. "That should do it. I'll return in ten minutes to help you clean it off." She stood to leave.

"Jude, look after him, won't you?" Nathan said quickly. "Peter, I mean. Counsel him where you're able. Correct him on the little things that my father's bound to notice."

She looked at him fondly. "Yes, of course."

After she left, he laid back on his pillows and closed his eyes. He thought of Peter visiting him, asking—without any sense of obligation—if he was all right. It was plain to see that he was a thoughtful person. Nathan very much wanted to call him his friend someday.

Suddenly, he was stirred from his reverie by quiet murmurs from the walls:

He is not gone. He waits. Watching.

A chill ran down Nathan's spine. He sat up and looked around his room. It was empty, but he knew that *he* wasn't gone. The man from the hallway. The one who moved through the house in utter darkness. The one with an unspeakable look in his eyes.

7

By the end of the day, Nathan's fever had improved considerably, and while it had not gone away entirely, it no longer required constant attention. Still, in an abundance of caution, Jude had arranged for Nathan to be accompanied throughout the night. Several staff members were to sit with him in one-hour shifts to keep watch, just in case his symptoms happened to take a turn for the worse.

It made Nathan feel like a child. He resented being treated like a delicate, helpless thing. However, another part of him acknowledged that he truly feared what may be awaiting him in the dark, so he did not object. Knowing that someone would be nearby while he slept was comforting.

Jude, of course, watched him for the first hour. "Goodnight, Nathan," she said before settling into an armchair at the far end of the room. Beside the chair stood a small end table with an oil lamp which aided her while she darned her stockings.

He fell asleep without any trouble and found himself in vague, unremarkable dreams that closely resembled the mundane affairs of his waking life. But there was something out of the ordinary. A presence. A tall, dark shape that resided in the shadows. At first, Nathan wasn't frightened by this; the figure stood far away, seeming to exist only in the periphery of his world. But, as the night continued and the course of his dreams shifted and changed, it drew nearer.

Dread slowly began to color Nathan's dreamscape. He found himself wandering in a bizarre maze of bleak, unwelcoming rooms, all of which appeared to be crude replicas taken from the summer home and his family's house in London. Though everything around him looked familiar, he was lost. There was no apparent exit, and he was alone. He tried doubling back at one point, but the rooms were not the same as they were when he left them, their layout and orientation apparently changing when he wasn't looking. Panic was beginning to set in.

Then, he heard the footsteps—the slow, heavy footsteps he'd heard the previous night outside of his chambers. It was the man from the hallway. Nathan could not see him, but he knew he was getting nearer. Nathan began to run.

The steps he heard behind him kept their slow, deliberate pace, yet they grew louder, closer. They became deafening. They could not be outrun. Suddenly, Nathan felt long, icy fingers clasp around his mouth from behind him.

He woke then, kicking and flailing violently in his bed, with a scream forming in the back of his throat.

"Nathan!"

He felt strong hands, broad and warm, placed firmly on his shoulders, unlike the ones belonging to the terrible man from his dreams. He stopped struggling.

The room was mostly dark, save for the dim light of the oil lamp next to the armchair. Nathan was sitting up in his bed now and glancing around wildly at the shadows in the corners of his chambers. They were empty.

"Nathan, are you all right?"

"Peter?" Nathan looked up to see the groundskeeper's face, lit by the soft glow of lamplight, staring worriedly back at him. "What are you doing here?"

"It's my hour to watch over you. You were starting to shout in your sleep. Is it the fever?" He put a hand to Nathan's brow. "You do feel warm. Should I get Mrs. Fairchild?"

"No, no. It's fine."

"Are you certain?"

"Yes. It was only a nightmare."

"Only a nightmare," Peter huffed. "Well, watching you have a nightmare is going to give *me* nightmares."

Nathan laughed at this, and Peter looked pleased with himself. The terror Nathan had felt only moments ago was becoming farther away now. "That's two nights in a row I've given you a scare, isn't it? I'm terribly sorry."

Peter shrugged amiably, "Serves me right, I suppose. I could be sleeping right now, but I chose to be here instead."

"You mean, you volunteered?"

"Sure. All of us did."

Nathan was surprised to learn this. He didn't imagine that anyone would've voluntarily chosen to lose an hour of sleep on his behalf. "That's very generous of you," he said. "I do hope I wasn't any trouble for the others."

"No, I don't believe so. It seemed that you were sleeping soundly before now. Just my luck, I guess," Peter said with a lopsided smile. "Are you feeling better?"

In truth, Nathan was feeling much better, but he also feared that the man from the hallway would return again, that he was merely awaiting him in sleep. "I am, yes. Thank you. I must admit, though, I'm worried I'll only have another nightmare if I fall asleep again."

"Do you get them often?"

"Not usually. However, after last night…" he trailed off, recalling the vision he'd had, the helpless terror he felt. He looked at Peter then. There was a calmness to his eyes that made the world around him seem less dire. It made Nathan feel safer, and in turn, braver.

"You said before that I looked terrified last night," Nathan continued, considering his next words with care so as not to reveal too much. "Well, I saw…a man outside of my door. A tall, imposing man with skin as pale as the whites of his eyes. Those terrible eyes… There wasn't any color to them at all. They were just black holes filled with nothing, not even a reflection. But they were opened wide in a manic sort of way and fixed directly on me."

Now, Peter's eyes were fixed on Nathan's, the crease between his brows revealing his concern.

“He came into the room, and I became petrified with fear,” Nathan said, speaking carefully to hide the tremble in his voice. “I felt then this sense that something unspeakable would befall me. Something worse than death. I was certain of it.

“My grasp failed me, and I dropped my candle. The darkness descended upon me like a weight, and I collapsed. I remember screaming and feeling his hands upon me. His cold fingers reaching for my mouth and throat…” he shuddered. “My next memory is that of a crowd of worried faces in my doorway and Jude looking down at me.”

“My God… It’s a wonder you didn’t die from fright!” Peter said.

“I worry that I might still. That man appeared in my dreams tonight. I’m afraid he’ll be there again when I close my eyes.”

“Don’t let him intimidate you,” Peter said with surprising seriousness. “He doesn't deserve the satisfaction. Should you see him again, tell him plainly to bugger off.”

Nathan thought about this for a moment and smiled weakly, “Perhaps, you’re right. At the very least, I suppose I can try.”

“If I can be frank, I get the sense that you’re more capable than you let yourself believe you are,” said Peter, not unkindly. “You shouldn’t doubt yourself.”

“Thank you,” Nathan said, and he meant it. “I feel rather fortunate that you happened to be here when I awoke.”

“I hope I helped,” Peter smiled, then glanced at the clock. “I should let you get back to sleep. If you need anything, I’ll be nearby.”

“Surely, you must be returning to bed soon.”

“I’m supposed to wake Mr. Millican at the hour—he’s got the last shift for the night—but I figured I’d let him sleep though. He needs it, and besides, it’s only one more hour. The house will start waking up then, and Mrs. Fairchild will be checking on you, I'm sure."

"Oh, I'd feel horrible to keep you awake!"

Peter just waved a hand. "It's no bother."

Nathan wanted to protest further, but in truth, he appreciated Peter's presence. It was oddly comforting. If he did have another bad dream, he wanted Peter to be there.

"Well, thank you. You really are too kind."

"Don't mention it," Peter smiled. "Goodnight, Nathan." With that, he stood up and walked back to the armchair.

"Goodnight, Peter."

Nathan settled back into his bed and felt comforted in knowing he wasn't alone. As he dozed back off, he thought then about what Peter had told him: *You're more capable than you let yourself believe you are.*

He wanted to believe that was true. He wanted to believe that he had it in him to face the man from his nightmares and tell him to go away. But the thought filled him with uneasiness.

How could he confront the looming figure that lived in the shadows? The one in the well-tailored suit with the terrible eyes. The one with his father's face.

8

The next morning, Nathan awoke surprisingly refreshed. His energy was beginning to return to him, and while he was certainly still on the mend, he was eager to leave the bed. He took a proper bath and shaved, giving the maids an opportunity to change his bed sheets which had grown dense with the smell of sweat and mustard.

Once clean, Nathan spent the day in the brilliant sunshine of the conservatory, propped up in an armchair with pillows, reading and napping between plasters. From where he sat, he could see Peter in the distance moving armfuls of dead plants from the greenhouse to a horse-drawn cart. He spent more time watching him that he cared to admit.

In addition to renewed energy, his appetite had also returned. For dinner that evening, he indulged in the biggest meal he'd eaten in days.

"I can't tell you how relieved we all are to see you're feeling better," Jude had said as Nathan was settling in for bed. She stayed with him again until he fell asleep, but after that, left him alone for the night. He didn't stir once.

The following day, Nathan felt better still, and his spirits were uplifted further by a letter from his mother. She told him enthusiastically about a recent trip to the opera house she'd made to see *Nell Gwynne*. Nathan smiled at this; his mother loved all forms of theater and could talk for hours on the subject.

Feeling well enough, he sat at his writing desk and composed a response to her, carefully leaving out any mention of his illness. She would only worry.

———

Dr. Beverley visited again at the end of the week. "My! You're looking a much healthier color since I last saw you," he said cheerily upon seeing Nathan. "You've made wonderful progress, lad. I best have a listen to your heart and lungs, just to be certain."

Nathan's daily life had mostly returned to normal. He was up and about again, and save for a lingering runny nose, he felt perfectly normal.

"It all sounds good," Dr. Beverley reported after a moment, removing the stethoscope from his ears. "But I like to hear it from the patient, too. How are you feeling? Is anything bothering you?"

"I'm feeling much better, doctor," he said. "I can't say I have any complaints, truthfully."

"Very good. That fever of yours didn't give you any more trouble, did it?"

"Thankfully, no. It was manageable."

"Excellent! Well, then I dare say that you no longer need me here," the doctor said, closing his medical bag. "Be sure that you don't overexert yourself for a few days more. Your body is still recovering after all. And one more suggestion, if I may… Spring will be here soon enough. Do not let it pass you by. I'm a firm believer that fresh air is good for the body and spirit alike. It is simple, honest medicine. Do you understand?"

"Yes, doctor, I believe I do," Nathan smiled.

"Good man. Should you or anyone here need me for anything, do not hesitate to call on me."

After Dr. Beverley left, Nathan returned to the conservatory. He'd spent most of his time there lately, in part because of the abundance of sunshine they'd been receiving over the past couple days. He settled down into his usual chair and tried continuing with his book, but it couldn't hold his attention. He glanced out of the window in front of him and watched the vague shape of Peter in the greenhouse.

"Good news from the doctor?" Jude asked, entering the room.

Nathan quickly looked back to his book, but Jude noticed. She looked out of the window to where he had been staring.

"It was," Nathan said. "Dr. Beverley said that I should continue to take things slow for another few days, but my heart and lungs sound normal. All is well."

"I'm glad to hear it," Jude said. She paused for a moment. "You know, Peter has been working tirelessly in that greenhouse. It must look drastically different than when he first arrived."

"Hm?" He looked up from his book reluctantly, as if absorbed. "Oh! Yes, of course. The greenhouse. I'm sure you're quite right, it must look very different."

"Perhaps it'd be worth a visit sometime when you're feeling up to it. To see how things are coming along."

"Maybe you're right. In fact, the doctor told me I needed more fresh air. That is as good an excuse as any, I suppose."

"Indeed," she said, looking well-pleased.

As the day continued and the sun fell closer to the horizon, Nathan knew that Peter would be coming in from the grounds soon. He pondered how he might get a moment with him to ask about visiting the greenhouse; he did not want to drop in unexpectedly as he had before.

However, Peter had no reason to be in the main part of the home. He would enter through the servants' entrance at the back of the house and remain out of sight. Similarly, Nathan had no reason to find himself in the servants' quarters. He supposed that he could have Jude relay the message to Peter for him, but he did not want to pass up an opportunity to talk with the groundskeeper himself.

After the sun had set, Nathan relocated to the library and continued to mull over how he might get a moment alone with Peter. Then, shortly before six o'clock, there was a knock at the door. To his great surprise, he turned to see Peter in the doorway.

"Peter? What are you—?"

"I'm sorry, I know I shouldn't be here," he said quickly. "I just wanted to see you for a moment to show you something I found while clearing out the hothouse." He hurried in and crouched next to Nathan's chair. From his pocket, he retrieved a smooth, flat stone that fit neatly in the palm of his hand. On the face of it, a crude "T" had been carved. "I didn't want to throw it out. I thought it might be a lost memento or something of the sort."

"Good heavens," Nathan said with wonder. He took the stone and examined it. "I haven't seen this in decades. My brother Daniel and I used to play together in the greenhouse when we were very young. We would make the other wait outside while we buried an old biscuit tin full of trinkets somewhere in one of the flowerbeds. Then, the other would try to find it. We'd use this stone to mark where it was buried. Daniel himself carved it. The 'T' stood for 'treasure.'"

"That makes sense. I found it in one of the flowerbeds, just like you said."

"I can hardly believe it's been found after all these years. It used to be my favorite game to play as a boy," he said wistfully. "Our mother hated it, though. We'd always come in covered in dirt, and she'd scold us for spoiling Mr. Millican's hard work."

It was then that he noticed that Peter had a smudge of dirt along the side of his face. "Speaking of," he added. "Looks like you've got a spot of dirt, just there on your cheek."

Embarrassed, Peter tried wiping it away but missed entirely. Nathan almost reached out a hand to clean it himself, then thought better of it.

"Did you find anything else in the greenhouse?" Nathan continued.

"No, only this," he said. "Do you think the biscuit tin is still in there as well?"

"I think it's very possible. Perhaps I could visit the greenhouse tomorrow, and we could have a look for it. I was wanting to see the progress you've made anyway. If that's fine with you, of course."

"Certainly," Peter smiled. "Can't say I've gone looking for buried treasure before. I'd be delighted." He looked over his shoulder. "I really should get going now, though. It's almost time for our dinner and if Mr. Millican finds me here, I'll be in hot water."

Peter left, and Nathan sat looking at the stone in his hands, turning it over and letting the memories come back to him. It struck him how much he missed the friendship he had with his brother Daniel when they were children. As they matured, they'd gradually grown apart. Daniel took an interest in business and investing, while Nathan preferred the arts. Despite their differences, they had always stayed considerate of each other, but they'd lost something they had together as boys.

Nathan hoped that he and Peter would find the old tin in the greenhouse tomorrow. It would make a wonderfully sentimental gift for Daniel, who would be visiting in the summer with their parents. He smiled at the thought.

9

"I found it just there."

Nathan stood with Peter as he pointed to where he discovered the stone the day before. It was another bright day, and though it was still cold outside, the greenhouse was warming up nicely in the late morning sun. The space itself had been completely transformed since Nathan's previous visit. The dead plants had all been removed from the garden beds, the walkways swept, the cobwebs cleared out, and the planters emptied and cleaned.

Peter had told him that he was nearly ready to cultivate the soil and introduce plants and seedlings. Before that could be done though, there remained one final task of locating long-lost treasure. With sleeves rolled up, they began digging around with hand trowels in the flowerbed.

Peter flashed Nathan a mischievous grin. "I take it whoever finds the treasure first gets to lay claim to the spoils?"

The challenge stirred a childlike excitement in Nathan. He hadn't felt so thrilled since he'd last hunted for treasure nearly twenty years ago in these very flowerbeds.

Without a word, he rammed his shoulder into Peter's and began digging in earnest. Peter responded in kind. They carried on nudging and elbowing each other, giggling like schoolboys, as they searched furiously for their prize.

Peter's trowel hit something solid, and he cried out. "Ha!"

He managed to grab the tin from the soil despite Nathan's efforts and lifted it victoriously over his head. Nathan lunged for it and sent them both toppling over into the dirt.

"Bless me!" Nathan scrambled to pull himself upright. "I'm so sorry, Peter. I got completely carried away! Are you all right?"

Peter was lying in the dirt, his face a giddy shade of pink, overcome with laughter. It was a new sound to Nathan; he very much liked it.

"You're certainly a gracious loser, aren't you?"

Nathan laughed now, too, and he helped him up. "I must say, I'm not usually such a competitive person," he said bashfully.

"Well, I'm glad I bring out the best in you," Peter grinned. "You're in quite a state, though."

Nathan looked down at himself. His white shirt was badly soiled. "Heaven help me, I am in for such a scolding. Mrs. Fairchild will never let me leave the house again. First the rain, now this."

"But I'd say it was worth it," said Peter, holding out the old biscuit tin to him.

"That's yours. You won it fairly."

"Oh, I couldn't possibly keep it," he insisted. "Go on then."

Nathan took the tin and wiped off the dirt from the top. It was badly rusted, but it was still intact, and with a bit of coaxing, the lid opened. Inside, they found a small collection of old toys and trinkets. Several marbles, a lead toy soldier, a spinning top, a silver sixpence, an oddly shaped river stone, and a small kaleidoscope.

"My God," he said softly. "I'd nearly forgotten about these. In fact, there's some I don't remember at all. They must have been Daniel's."

"May I?"

Nathan set the tin between them, and Peter delicately lifted the kaleidoscope out as if he was handling artifacts from an archaeological dig site. He closed one eye and looked through the eyehole, carefully turning the small wheel of stained glass on the front end.

"Fantastic!" he exclaimed. "I've always wanted to look through one of these."

Nathan watched in amusement as the groundskeeper marveled at the kaleidoscope. Peter was honest and unabashed in his excitement. Nathan admired it.

"It's absolutely wonderful," he continued. "Have a look."

Nathan had played with it many times as a child, but he indulged him anyway. He held up the kaleidoscope to his eye and was treated to a starburst of colors and light. It really was wonderful, he thought. As he turned the stained-glass wheel, the pattern changed before his eyes, and the colors were practically singing. It was more magical than Nathan remembered; it was positively captivating.

"What's that?" Peter asked then.

"Hm?"

"That song you were humming just now."

Nathan looked at him and blinked. "Oh, sorry. I hadn't realized I was."

Peter studied him for a moment. "You know, you're a bit of a funny one," he mused. "But it was nice, whatever it was. Something about it reminded me of when I was a boy."

"Perhaps a nursery rhyme," Nathan offered, but he was anxious to change the subject. "Ah! Look here. This," he plucked a glass marble from the tin, "was my favorite marble. The ones made from actual marble are better quality, of course, but I always preferred the glass ones. I thought they looked like gems."

"They certainly look appropriate for a treasure chest," Peter agreed.

"What about you? What were some of your favorite toys?"

Peter took a sudden interest in his hands. "Ah, well, growing up on a farm, I didn't have toys that came from the shops."

"I see," Nathan said understandingly. "But you must have kept yourself entertained somehow. What sorts of things did you do?"

He shrugged. "There was always something that needed doing on the farm. I was busy a lot of the time." A memory appeared to come to him then, and he became more animated. "Although, I would sometimes play in the barn's hayloft. I remember having the most fun up there. I'd run and jump into the hay pile or climb to the top and slide down. And sometimes, I would burrow into it and imagine I was digging to the other side of the world." Peter was grinning at the memory, and Nathan smiled, too.

"I feel I can picture in my head what you must have been like as a child," he told him.

"Well, I don't have to imagine what *you* were like," Peter teased, reaching out and brushing some of the dirt from Nathan's shirt. The contact startled Nathan, but Peter didn't notice. "So, what'll you be doing with all this?"

"Oh, um…" Nathan cleared his throat. "I was thinking I would give it to my brother as a gift when he comes to visit in the summer with my parents. He's got a birthday in September. They'll be gone by then, of course. But I figured I would give it to him before they leave."

"Can't you make a trip home for his birthday? You talk as if you're trapped here."

Nathan avoided his eyes and said nothing.

A look of worry grew on Peter's face. "*Are* you trapped here?"

Before he could respond, the greenhouse door opened abruptly, and Mr. Millican shuffled in with a sense of urgency.

"Master Nathan, you've got— Oh my word! Your shirt, sir! Peter, why on earth is Master Nathan sitting in a flowerbed?"

"It's my fault, Mr. Millican," Nathan said. "Peter was merely showing me the greenhouse, and I took a bit of a fall. But I'm quite all right. Now, what have you come to tell me?"

"You've got a visitor, sir. He's in the house now."

Peter stood and gave a hand to Nathan.

"I'm not expecting anyone. Who is it?"

"Dr. Mathis, sir."

The blood drained from Nathan's face. "Here? Wh-What is he doing here?"

"I'm not certain, sir. But he said he's here to see you and that Lady Hambleton sent him."

"Mother sent him?"

"Yes, sir, that's right. And he seems to think he's spending the night here. He brought a suitcase."

"Who is Dr. Mathis?" Peter asked.

Mr. Millican's mouth went tight. "I daresay that's none of your business," he snapped. "Now, Master Nathan, I can take you through the servants' entrance so you can get to your chambers and change your shirt. I'll let the doctor know that you'll be with him shortly."

Nathan followed him out of the greenhouse, leaving behind Peter with the tin of found treasure. He glanced back and saw Peter, still standing in the flowerbed and looking at him with a worried expression. Nathan gave him a smile that he hoped was reassuring.

As they crossed the grounds towards the house, Nathan glanced to the horizon and saw a blanket of clouds stretching towards the estate. Their spell of fair weather was over.

10

Dr. Mathis was waiting in the parlor. He was a tall man with short, graying hair that was always impeccably combed to one side. On the bridge of his thin, straight nose sat a small pair of glasses that he would often look over the top of with his sunken, uninterested eyes.

"Dr. Mathis," Nathan said, entering the room in a clean shirt with Jude at his heels. "What an unexpected surprise. It's wonderful to see you."

He looked over his glasses at Nathan, studying him briefly. Then, he turned his gaze to Jude and spoke, "I'm not sure why my arrival should come as a surprise. Lady Hambleton said she informed the housekeeper I'd be coming." The doctor spoke slowly and without warmth. Nathan had always hated the sound of his voice.

"We haven't received a telegram from Lady Hambleton, doctor," Jude said nervously. "If she sent a letter, it appears you made it here first. But it's no trouble at all, sir. We'll have a room made up for you in no time."

"I'm sure you will," he said flatly.

"To what do we owe the pleasure of your company, doctor?" Nathan said.

"Your mother sent me. Asked me to see you right away. She said your condition has not improved since you've been here."

"Oh? I'm not sure I follow you."

"You don't? Are you in denial about your health, or are you being deliberately obtuse?"

"No! I'm not— It's not that I'm—" he stammered. "I'm not in denial. I'm just unsure what would have led my mother to that assumption."

"Persistent headaches, reckless behavior, outbursts in the night," Dr. Mathis rattled off. "This certainly does not sound like improvement to me."

"Reckless—? What?" Nathan was confused and becoming increasingly anxious. He had not mentioned his health to his mother since he'd arrived at the summer home. "I-I do still get headaches sometimes, but they're minor."

"Nathaniel, we have been through this before," Dr. Mathis sighed. "Attempting to minimize your ailments does not make them go away."

"I'm not attempting to minimize," he insisted. "I really have been doing much better since leaving London, I assure you."

"Is that so? As I understand it, you wandered out of the house into the freezing rain, without a word to anyone or even a jacket. Is that right?"

"W-Well, yes, but—"

"Your carelessness earned you a cold. And, then you woke the entire house by screaming in the dead of night."

These were details his mother could not have possibly known, Nathan thought. He glanced at Jude. With her head hung low, she avoided his gaze. He felt a deep hurt within him then, a terrible pain that struck him in his gut and gripped his heart. His eyes stung with tears.

"That was a fever," he tried to assert, but his voice was threatening to break.

"Maybe so, but we cannot pretend that you do not have a history of outbursts. You can try to blame your fever for this incident, but what about before?"

Nathan said nothing. He could not, for there was a tightness in his throat, and he feared that if he opened his mouth he may start to cry.

"I see you're upset," Dr. Mathis said mildly. "I was afraid my visit would create too much excitement for you, and I can see that it has. Take a rest, and we can continue this conversation after dinner. I don't mean to rush the matter, but I've come here on short notice, and I must leave first thing in the morning."

Nathan gave a small, pathetic nod and left the parlor. He heard Jude speaking behind him, telling the doctor to make himself comfortable and that she would send the footman to let him know when his room was ready.

He was halfway to his chambers when heard the hurried steps of Jude approaching behind him. "Nathan, I'm so sorry, I—"

"That's all for now, Mrs. Fairchild," he said tightly, without sparing her a glance.

"But if I could only explain—"

"I said that's all."

The sound of Jude's steps stopped. Nathan marched forward, his eyes burning again with fresh tears.

———

In his room, he hadn't been able to rest at all. There'd been too many thoughts in his mind and too much hurt in his heart. That Jude, his best friend, would betray him was unbelievable. Yet she had. He was as angry as he had ever been, but even more than that, he was grief-stricken. Even in the midst of his heartache, he could not imagine his life without Jude in it.

Later that evening, after an uncomfortably silent dinner, Nathan and Dr. Mathis reconvened in the library to continue with their earlier conversation.

"You were sent here to care for your health, and from what I've heard, it has not gotten better."

"I wasn't sent here for my health. I was banished to this place," Nathan muttered.

Dr. Mathis sighed. "Must you be so dramatic?"

"Perhaps that is all that's wrong with me."

"I'm sure you wish that were the case," he quipped. "But, for as long as I've known you, you've had a weak constitution. There's no wishing it away. I'm worried now, though, that your condition is progressive."

"What do you mean?"

"Well, there are others in this world with health sensitivities like yourself. Some are able to adapt to their limitations and live relatively normal lives. For others, their ailments are more severe and worsen as time goes on, making adaptation impossible. I'm afraid you may be the latter."

"What?" Nathan asked, alarmed. "But nothing has changed, I'm the same as I've always been."

"From your perspective, perhaps. But I'm inclined to disagree. This sort of diagnosis can take years to ascertain, because a child needs to grow before one can tell whether their symptoms are manageable. Children tend to experience things more acutely; however, over time, they become familiar with their afflictions. They learn how to adjust and cope with them, and so their symptoms appear to resolve to some degree as they reach adulthood. This is the case for the first group I mentioned.

"Now, consider your own situation. If your ailments are as intense for you now as an adult as they were when you were a child, then it stands to reason that your condition is worsening as you age, rendering it unmanageable. If this wasn't the case, you would have shown greater improvement by this point."

"But I have improved!" Nathan said desperately. "I'm much better than when I was young. I am!"

"You say this, but yet the smallest bit of excitement disturbs you. Christmas Day gave you a debilitating headache. A cold sends you into a fit of hysterics. And just today, I learned that you couldn't even be trusted to take a simple stroll through the greenhouse without ruining your clothes. Your estate manager said he found you in a flowerbed, covered in dirt. A dizzy spell, was it?"

Nathan did not correct him on this, because the truth—that he was looking for long-forgotten childhood treasure—would only sound more preposterous. When he said nothing, the doctor continued.

"It seems impossible to know exactly what will upset you, and therein lies the problem. If it's not a holiday or a simple outing, then it's something else entirely—like electric lights. This makes treatment and prevention exceedingly difficult."

At the mention of electric lights, Nathan winced and lowered his head. Still, he kept quiet.

"Truthfully, I want to believe you when you say you're making progress," Dr. Mathis said. "Every doctor wants their patients to get better. But it is hard to contend with evidence."

An old, familiar hopelessness found Nathan. He knew it was pointless to argue. He knew his words held no credibility. It was the same as it had always been.

With his hands in his lap, he stared blankly at the floor in front of him. "Then what is your recommendation, doctor?"

"Well," the doctor stood and poured himself a brandy from the nearby table, "To start, you will establish a routine of utmost consistency. I feel that predictability is paramount to your wellbeing. That means no visitors, no outings, no celebrations, no surprises of any kind. You are to live as simply as possible."

"For how long?"

"At the very least, until I visit again to check on your progress. I'll return the first week in May."

"*May?*" he said incredulously. "But, that's six weeks from now."

"Yes, I'm aware," Dr. Mathis replied, looking pointedly at Nathan over his glasses. "Lifestyle changes such as these need an adequate trial to judge their effectiveness."

"And I'm not allowed to leave the house in that time? But the village doctor said that I needed more fresh air."

"Then open a window." Dr. Mathis's patience was running thin. "You do not sound committed to getting better, Nathaniel. You do want to get better, don't you?"

Nathan thought suddenly of his mother and his father and of all the friends throughout his life who never stayed his friend for long. Then, he thought of Peter and realized all at once how desperately he did, in fact, want to get better. He wanted to put an end to the unwelcome visions no one else saw and voices no one else heard. And, while he didn't feel confident in Dr. Mathis's methodology, he had to be willing to try.

"Yes, I do, doctor," he said quietly.

"Good. Then you realize, of course, that this may be a solution. What will initially start as a trial may become permanent if I find that it improves your condition."

"And if it doesn't?"

Dr. Mathis seemed to debate answering the question, looking uncharacteristically sympathetic. "There are more aggressive forms of treatment," he said finally. "Hydropathy, for example. As well as sedatives and regular observation…"

Nathan felt a chill in his heart. He understood the implication, but still, he wanted to hear it from the doctor. "You mean, an asylum?"

"Yes."

At the doctor's reply, a noise erupted in the room; a chattering sound, a deafening cacophony of murmurs and mutters that frantically circled the room in desperate warning. Dr. Mathis seemed not to hear it, so Nathan did his best to appear as though he didn't either. No sooner had the noise arose than it stopped, leaving the room in tense silence once again.

"I do hope it doesn't come to that," Dr. Mathis said, as if nothing had transpired. "Mind you, if it does, it needn't be forever. Perhaps, only a few months—maybe more. It all depends how soon you respond to treatment."

"Yes, doctor, I understand," he said absently.

"But we mustn't get ahead of ourselves. We shall proceed with this trial first. I'll speak with your estate manager and housekeeper tomorrow before I leave to ensure that they understand what I expect for the next six weeks. Until then, I must retire."

Dr. Mathis left Nathan alone with his thoughts. He didn't know how long he remained there on the sofa, grappling with the weight of the conversation he'd just had. The familiar hopelessness had set further into his bones and made him unwilling to move. At some point, he found himself back in his chambers, but the memory of how he got there was hazy; he could vaguely remember the footman finding him in the library and ushering him through the house.

In his room, Nathan sat on the edge of his bed and buried his face into his hands. He felt certain he would begin crying, but no tears came.

11

Sometime later, there came a knock at the door. Nathan didn't respond, but still, the door opened anyway.

He lifted his head to see Jude standing in the doorway. Her eyes were red and wet. In her hands, she held the biscuit tin he'd found in the greenhouse earlier that day with Peter. That felt like a lifetime ago now.

He wanted to tell her to go away, that he didn't want to speak with her, but he wanted to know why she had the tin with her. So, he waited for her to speak.

"I'm sorry. Peter asked me to give this to you. I told him he could bring it to you himself, but he insisted I do it."

When Nathan still said nothing, she walked in and set the tin on the nearby table.

"I know you must think I'm awful," she said. "I should've told you. I don't know why I didn't."

"Told me what, Mrs. Fairchild? That you lied about being my friend, so you could spy on me for my mother?"

"No!" She looked shocked. "Is that really what you think?"

"It's the truth, isn't it?"

"Nathan, I've never lied about being your friend. I would never do anything so repugnant."

"Yet, you contacted my mother without my knowing. And God only knows what you've told her, but it clearly caused her enough concern to send Dr. Mathis here and have him discuss the possibility of me being committed to a bedlam!" He was speaking as loudly as he dared, knowing that Dr. Mathis was still in the house. "Tell me, Mrs. Fairchild, what *is* your definition of the word friend?"

Jude was beginning to cry. "I had to! Don't you understand? Your mother has always requested that I write to her, for as long as I have worked here! Every month, she expects correspondence from me, updating her on the affairs of the home while they're in London. Since you've arrived, I've still written to her as I always have, but now she asks after you. She wants to know you're all right."

"Don't lie to me. Why wouldn't Mr. Millican write to my father directly regarding the affairs of the estate?"

"He does. But your mother isn't interested in matters of business or finance. She writes to me to know that the staff is content and to ensure that the home is properly prepared for their arrival in summer."

"Fine, but you didn't have to tell her everything."

"I don't!" She was almost shouting now herself. "But I can't hide everything either! If there is something that the entire house knows about, I can't keep that a secret from her. Everyone knew of your headache during Christmas, and everyone was awoken by your fever. I cannot exclude these things from my letters. If she were to somehow find out that I neglected to tell her these things, that I hid them from her, I could lose my job. And this is all that I have."

A silence grew between them. Nathan had deflated; Jude sat in a nearby armchair and blotted her eyes.

"How would the truth ever get back to her?" Nathan asked finally, in a weak attempt to prod the argument.

She shot him an annoyed look over her handkerchief before wiping her nose. "Don't be naïve. You know servants gossip. Your mother will be accompanied by her lady's maid this summer, same as she always is. And, that woman is an absolute church bell. If anyone here said something in passing, she'd tell your mother in a heartbeat."

"Then, what did you say that made her worried enough to send Dr. Mathis?"

"Truthfully, I don't know," Jude said, seeming at a loss. "I never tell her more than I feel I have to. And, in fact, I usually tell her of things once they've resolved, so she doesn't have reason to worry. I wrote to her about your cold only after you started recovering. But, I suppose, mothers will fret regardless."

Nathan stared at his hands and thought about what Jude had said. He understood her predicament and found some relief in learning that she was not, after all, a heartless person. Even still, a part of him felt wounded.

"I wish you had just told me," he said.

"I know," she said apologetically. "I really am so sorry. Honestly, I didn't think there was any harm in it. I was just writing to Lady Hambleton, same as I always had. It was careless, though. I see that now. I just never imagined she would do something like this."

Nathan thought then about why he'd been sent away from his home in London. That night in October. The electric lights. The outburst.

"Perhaps, it's not so surprising that she's as sensitive as she is," he admitted. "She never told you the details of why I was sent here, did she?"

"She didn't," Jude said. "And I won't pry."

"Thank you. I'm sure I will tell you someday, but I just need some time."

"I understand." She got up and walked to sit beside him on the bed. "Now, what's this about Dr. Mathis mentioning an asylum?"

The rawness Nathan felt in the wake of his argument with Jude coalesced with the fear inside him from his conversation with Dr. Mathis. The tears finally came to him then. He rested his head on Jude's shoulder and started to cry.

He told her through choked sobs about their conversation and how he only had six weeks to convince Dr. Mathis that being committed wasn't necessary.

"He said, for the next six weeks, he doesn't want me doing anything. I can't even leave the house. I might as well be incarcerated."

"My God, this is all my fault." Jude was visibly distressed. "This all happened because of my letters. Nathan, I can't tell you how sorry I am."

He looked at her with swollen, red eyes and shook his head. "You had a responsibility to tell her. What choice did you have?"

"I suppose you're right… But your mother will continue to expect future correspondence from me. Perhaps, we should draft those letters together from now on."

Nathan smiled weakly. "It might not matter soon enough."

"Don't talk like that," she said firmly, wrapping a secure arm around his shoulder. "You won't be committed. I won't allow it."

He wanted to feel comforted by that, but in truth, he felt only despondent. "I'm sorry I was so spiteful before," he said. "I made terrible accusations."

"The past is what it is. It doesn't serve us to dwell on it."

They sat together in silence as the events of the evening settled around them like dust. Nathan was glad to have Jude as his friend again, but fear of the future weighed on him. It seemed the more he thought about it, the harder it was to muster any optimism at all.

He noticed the biscuit tin on the table and thought of Peter. A lightness fluttered in his chest, and for a moment, he almost smiled to himself at the memory of digging in the flowerbed. But then he remembered the shirt he soiled and the words of Dr. Mathis.

You couldn't even be trusted to take a simple stroll through the greenhouse without ruining your clothes.

Nathan thought to himself that he would always be a disappointment to those around him. He had known for many years that he would never meet the expectations the world had of him as Viscount Hambleton's son, and consequently, he would forever live his life under scrutiny. In this, he discovered a bitter irony—mistakes and shortcomings built upon each other, so the longer the world watched him, the less it seemed to like him. Now, every step out of line was another unforgivable failure, further damaging his already poor reputation and robbing him of any credibility he may have still possessed.

If the world at large believed one man to be worthless, Nathan thought, it would be senseless to deny it.

12

Dr. Mathis left by midmorning but not before informing Jude and Mr. Millican of Nathan's schedule prescription. They were told to do everything in their power to uphold the sanctity of his daily routine.

Nathan did not see Dr. Mathis off. He could not bring himself to leave his bed. Jude had lied on his behalf and told the doctor that he was still recovering from the excitement of the day before, which Nathan supposed wasn't a total lie.

When the doctor was gone, Jude visited him in his chambers.

"I'm afraid there's not much we can do about the next six weeks. Mr. Millican and I have been instructed to tell the rest of the staff about your treatment. I can't ask Mr. Millican to ignore the doctor's orders and betray Lady Hambleton's wishes. But you and I will figure out some way to make this bearable."

"I do appreciate your tenacity. But don't worry yourself," he said from beneath his blankets. "What difference does it make if I can't leave the house? I haven't hardly left since arriving here anyway."

Nathan found that he didn't have an appetite and skipped both breakfast and lunch. Late in the day, he finally dressed and left his room, but it took considerable effort.

The staff treated him differently. They watched him carefully and tried to move as quietly as possible in his presence, as if the sound of their footsteps would disturb him. He tried not to notice.

At first, he sat in the conservatory, but it was raining and looking through the windows was like looking at the world with watery eyes. He then tried reading in both the parlor and the library, but they reminded him of his conversation with Dr. Mathis. In the end, he went back to his chambers and into his bed.

Jude brought supper to his room that evening, and though he wasn't hungry, he ate enough to appease her. Then, he retired for the night. It was surprising to him how tired he felt; even after spending the majority of the day in bed, he was utterly enervated. It was an exhaustion he felt deep in the fiber of his muscles and made his own limbs cumbersome. He closed his eyes and quickly surrendered to sleep.

The days that followed were more of the same. Nathan would wake up feeling tired still, lie in bed for most of the morning, and then plod around the house long enough for the maids to clean his chambers.

The rain persisted. His appetite remained scarce. And Jude appeared obviously concerned. But so long as Nathan made an effort with dinner and left his room at least once a day, she refrained from commenting on his behavior.

———

One morning, Nathan was awoken early by Jude marching brightly into his room and drawing back his curtains.

"Look! The sun is shining!"

He groaned and buried his face into the pillow. She responded by pulling the blankets off him.

"It would be a lovely day to sit in the conservatory. Plenty of sunshine and warmth. Just the thing to lift your spirits."

"Who said my spirits needed lifting?" he muttered, squinting from the light.

She walked to his wardrobe and started pulling out clothes for him to wear. "I've let you mope around as much as you like for the past week. It's time now, though, for you to get some fresh air like Dr. Beverley said. We'll open the windows. It's mild today."

"But Jude, that might prove to be too much excitement for me," he snarked.

She put a hand on her hip and warned him, "If you're not out of bed before breakfast this morning, I'll show you excitement."

Not willing to call her bluff, Nathan pulled himself from bed and dressed. He did everything at a sluggish pace these days, but he thought it was just as well. It wasn't as if he had any reason to hurry.

In the conservatory, the large windows were opened, and the space was flooded with sunlight and spring air. It was a welcome change, and Nathan found that it did, in fact, lift his spirits. For the first time in days, he was able read his book, rather than just stare at words on a page.

He read a chapter or two but then stopped to take in the day outside. All the trees on the property were beginning to sprout vibrant, young leaves at the ends of their branches, and the lawn was looking especially lush after the rain. A delicate choir of birdsong filled the air, accompanied by the smell of dew wafting through the windows. He closed his eyes and took a deep breath.

He heard hooves then and opened his eyes to see the stableman in the distance, riding one the horses with a cart in tow. He parked it near the greenhouse, and a moment later, Peter came out of the barn. Together they unhitched the cart, pulled the tarp off the top, and began unloading plants of different shapes and sizes into the greenhouse.

At the sight of Peter, Nathan became more alert, and an idea came to him suddenly that he should go out and help them. Then he remembered his prescription. For a moment, he considered if there was some way he could leave the house without anyone noticing, but he knew it was risky. The staff was told to keep a watchful eye on him, and he knew that any misstep would get back to Dr. Mathis. Even though Nathan trusted that Peter wouldn't tell anyone if he left the house, he knew the stableman would.

Dr. Mathis's words returned to him.

This may be a solution... What will start as a trial may become permanent.

The energy that had found him before disappeared again, leaving him feeling heavy and dispirited. He knew his own wants and desires would never matter more than his family's. One way or another, he would live the rest of his life in captivity.

No longer able to bear looking out on the world he would never have a place in, he stood up and made for his room. He came across Jude in the hall who looked surprised to see him. She stopped and appeared on the verge of a question, but he kept walking and muttered as he passed, "I tried. I'm sorry."

She did not follow him or press him further.

When Nathan reached his chambers and crawled back into his bed, the murmurs began. Quiet voices whispering terrible, hopeless things in his ear. He tried escaping them—burying his head beneath his blankets and pillows, covering his ears with his hands—but nothing helped. And the more he struggled to escape the sound, the more fatigued he felt. After some time, he finally gave up.

He laid there and listened.

13

As the day pressed on, so too did the whispers. The words began repeating in Nathan's head like a mantra of misery and self-loathing.

He skipped dinner much to Jude's disapproval, but he sent her away and went to bed early. Despite the voices, he was finally able to fall asleep; however, it was a short-lived victory, because *he* was there, waiting for Nathan in the shadows of his dreams with wild, empty eyes.

In his nightmares, Nathan tried to find the courage to face the dark figure of his father and tell him to leave, but his throat had gone dry, and his words wouldn't come. As the phantom drew nearer with hands outstretched, Nathan tried to scream; he tried to fight. But he was powerless.

A cold hand covered his mouth. Hollow, black eyes stared into his, only inches away. Nathan watched in silent horror as a spindly finger raised to the man's pale, dried lips.

Shhh.

Nathan woke in a panic, his sweat-soaked nightshirt clinging to his skin, but he found no relief from the terror of his dreams. In the darkness, he felt something in the room with him. As quickly as he could, he scrambled out of bed, lit the oil lamp, and looked frantically around at the darkest corners of the room. They appeared empty. But he knew he was not alone. The weight of watching eyes was heavy upon him.

With the light from the lamp as only a mild comfort, he returned to his bed and sat in the unnatural stillness that pervaded his chambers. Even the whispering had stopped. All that was left was maddening silence.

He spent the rest of the night awake, watching the shadows closely, afraid to take his eyes off them for too long. The first light of day came hours later, and for the first time all night, Nathan felt truly relieved. He allowed himself to lay down and close his eyelids, but just as he approached the edge of sleep, the whispering returned. He tossed and turned, frustrated beyond belief, wishing desperately that they would leave him alone, but they never did.

It was another two hours before his exhaustion overtook him, and despite the susurrus he finally fell asleep. No sooner had he dozed off than Jude knocked on the door and entered to wake him for the day. His blood boiled in an instant.

How could she be so inconsiderate? He was so tired, and he'd only just gotten to sleep. Was she trying to upset him?

"Good morning. Are you feeling any—?"

"Goddammit, leave me alone!"

She gaped at him with wide eyes, stunned. The sound of his own voice had surprised him.

"Jude, I'm so sorry," he said remorsefully, pressing his palms to his eyes. "Really, I am. I haven't slept at all, and I'm just so tired… I don't feel like myself. Please, forgive me. I'll be all right, I just need sleep."

"Of course…"

Jude left without another word, and Nathan berated himself. He felt like yelling. And crying. But he wouldn't let himself do either.

Pulling the blankets over his head, he shut his eyes and relented to the sound of the terrible whispers. It was useless to resist them; he didn't have the strength. So, he admitted defeat and let them stay.

The days that followed were the darkest Nathan had ever known. Throughout the nights, he stayed awake with his oil lamp lit, watching the shadows, keeping an eye out for anything that may be lurking in them. When the sun rose, he slept as best he could despite the incessant voices in his head. He woke late in the day and left his room long enough for the maids to clean. Though he lived as a recluse, he did make a weak effort to keep up appearances with the staff.

Jude said little to Nathan but did cover for his behavior without him asking. She told the staff that Master Nathan had taken his prescription to heart and, as such, decided to spend the majority of his time in the tranquility of his room. She personally shuttled meals from the kitchen to his chambers so that no one else would discover that he was actually sleeping the days away. Nathan, of course, usually slept through both breakfast and lunch, and Jude would discreetly dispose of the food he didn't eat. She also refilled the lamp in his room herself so no one would question how much oil he was burning.

In two weeks' time, Nathan had lost a considerable amount of weight, and his eyes had dark circles beneath them. He felt constantly lethargic, his nerves were in shambles, and he'd lost track of the days of the week. He didn't know how much longer he could survive like this. He thought back to October, remembering how miserable he had been for so many weeks leading up to his outburst. At this rate, he was bound to have another, which would—without a doubt—be the final nail in his coffin. The bedlam awaited.

Jude showed increasing concern, but she continued to tread lightly around him and said little. One evening as she was leaving with his dinner tray, she turned to him and said, "Peter's been asking about you. He said he no longer sees you reading in the conservatory and asked me if you'll be all right. I wish I knew what to tell him." And, without another word, she left him for the night.

Nathan's chest ached at the thought of Peter. He had sincerely believed that they were on the path to becoming friends, but now, he knew it was a lost cause. He knew that he had no future at all.

A terrible thought came to him then. A thought that frightened him more than any of the voices or nightmares that had tormented him. He pushed it from his mind as quickly as it could, but the idea had already taken root—

If life ever became completely unbearable, he could always put an end to it himself.

14

Mr. Millican fell in mid-April. He'd been in the stairwell in the servants' quarters and earned a broken lower leg and sprained wrist. As soon as he was discovered, he was rushed to the village where he was seen by Dr. Beverley. The doctor bandaged his wrist and plastered his leg, but he worried that Mr. Millican may have hit his head as well. So, he kept him most of the day for observation.

Eventually, Mr. Millican was released back to the summer home with the explicit instruction to rest. He would have to wait for his wrist to heal completely before he could begin using crutches. Despite having survived the ordeal and being given an optimistic prognosis from Dr. Beverley, Mr. Millican despaired.

He told Jude, "Men my age don't recover from something like this. Not fully. This may be the beginning of the end."

She told him not to think that way, to keep his spirits up, but he began preparing for the worst. He wrote to Lord Hambleton informing him of the accident and swiftly received a letter in return stating that Lord and Lady Hambleton would *not* be seeking a replacement for him as they both expected him to make a full recovery.

In the meantime, Mr. Millican delegated his duties among the staff while he recovered and gave Peter the task of closing the house at night before bed—ensuring that the doors were locked, the fires had been snuffed out, and the windows were secured. He wanted to familiarize the groundskeeper with the house, in case his own health continued to worsen and the staff needed additional help indoors.

Nathan learned of this arrangement that night when he heard a knock on his door at an unusually late hour.

"Peter?" He sat up in surprise at seeing him in the doorway.

"Sorry, I hope I didn't wake you. Mr. Millican asked me to close the house for the night, and I just need to make sure your windows are secure."

For the first time in weeks, Nathan smiled. "You don't have to check the ones in occupied bedrooms."

The groundskeeper looked mortified. "Oh God, I'm so sorry. Mr. Millican didn't say. This is my first time."

"That's quite all right," he said reassuringly. "It's nice to see you, anyway."

Peter glanced back at the door for a moment as if debating whether to leave or not. Then he gestured to a nearby chair, "May I?"

"Certainly."

He pulled the chair over to the side of the bed and examined Nathan more closely in the lamplight. "My word, what's happened to you? You look like you've lost a stone since I saw you last."

Nathan thought about lying. He was ashamed of the truth and didn't want Peter to think differently of him. But it was pointless to postpone the inevitable. He had known that it was only a matter of time before Peter learned enough about his condition to change his opinions of him.

"I'm not sleeping well," he told him simply. "I stay up all night and try to sleep during the day, but I'm always tired. More tired than I am hungry."

"I don't understand. You seemed fine in the greenhouse. Who was that Dr. Mathis?"

"My family's doctor. He's been caring for me since I was a child. I've never much liked him though, if I'm honest."

"Why won't he let you leave the house or have visitors? Are you ill?"

"He thinks I am." He fidgeted with the hem of the blanket. "In fact, I'm quite certain he thinks I'm a lunatic. And, as of late, I'm starting to believe him."

Peter eyed him suspiciously. "Why would he think that?"

Nathan swallowed, the truth teetering precariously on the tip of his tongue. Once he admitted to his ailments, he wouldn't be able to take the words back. There was still time to lie, he thought. But there was something morbid in him that wanted to hear Peter's rejection, to confirm all the horrible things that the whispers said about him. For the past few weeks, he felt that he was at the lowest point of his life, and he didn't care anymore if he went lower.

"I hear and see things that aren't there."

He waited for something drastic to happen—for Peter to leave abruptly, for Dr. Mathis to appear suddenly and send him away to an asylum, for the world around him to fall apart entirely—but everything was surprisingly calm. Peter merely looked at him with interest.

"What sorts of things?"

"Oh, um…" He hadn't expected the conversation to continue. "I'd rather not talk about it."

"Sorry, my curiosity got the better of me. But is it frightening? Having visions?"

Nathan could hardly believe he was having this conversation. "Lately, it has been, but it isn't always."

"And so, is that why you're here all alone, without your family?"

"Well, yes, but it's more than just that…" Nathan took a breath. "My affliction makes me very sensitive at times, and last year, at our home in London, I had a rather dramatic outburst that led to an altercation of sorts. My father was at his wits' end. So, he sent me here."

"For how long?"

He shrugged. "I suppose until they think I'm well enough to return. But they heard that I woke the house in a screaming fit recently, which they've taken as a sign that I'm still unwell."

"But that was only a fever."

"I'm afraid they don't see it that way."

"Does your family also think you're mad, then? What about your friends?"

"My father certainly does. I always thought my mother believed me to be sane. But she was the one who sent Dr. Mathis, so now I'm not so sure." He cleared his throat uncomfortably, "As for friends, I haven't got any."

Nathan felt Peter's eyes on him, but he couldn't meet them with his own.

"I have a hard time believing that."

"I have Jude," he admitted, "but I've been so terrible lately, we've started growing apart... In general, I've never had much luck with friends. It seems no matter how hard I try to hide my peculiarities, they inevitably make themselves known and scare people away. I end up doing something that puts them off or mentioning something that I shouldn't know."

"Like, Violet."

Nathan finally looked at Peter who stared back with an unreadable expression. "Yes, like that," he said hesitantly. "What does Violet mean?"

"You mean, you don't know?" he asked, surprised.

"No. I often don't with these things. I may get a word or two, and that's all."

Peter studied him for a moment and then said, "Violet is my mother's name. She also knows things without being told. Like you do." He smiled then as Nathan looked at him with total astonishment. "She's always had it, even when she was a girl. She just knows little things before you tell her or gets hunches about people that always prove to be accurate. I don't think it's ever frightening for her, though."

Nathan's mind was overwhelmed with dozens of thoughts and questions all at once. He'd never known someone to have the same affliction as him. From the sound of it, though, Peter's mother wouldn't define it as a malady. Though, perhaps she might. Maybe she was also tortured by the things she experienced but hid her suffering well. Maybe she was as deranged as he was and simply didn't care. Nathan imagined a tired-looking woman with features reminiscent of Peter's, confined to her bed, kept up at night by horrible visions and voices; a woman who spoke with a sad, pained smile in the company of others and insisted that she was fine whenever asked.

"What's she like?"

"She's not a lunatic if that's what you're asking," Peter smirked. "She is a wonderful woman. Strong, compassionate. Always busy with something, but never in a hurry. She puts people off sometimes, because they can tell that she really *sees* them and they don't like it. But she's got a truly wonderful heart."

"So, that's where you got yours from," Nathan said without pausing to think if it was a good idea.

Peter smiled bashfully and looked away.

"She does sound wonderful," Nathan added quickly. In fact, Violet sounded like the antithesis of the woman he imagined. It made a part of him feel hopeful, that someone like him could be strong and confident and happy. "Has she ever told you where her insights come from?"

"No," he shook his head. "Like you, she doesn't like to talk about it directly. But she always said to me that if I ever heard or saw something I couldn't explain, I shouldn't fear it. Nor should I doubt my senses."

Nathan smiled ruefully. "That's just the opposite of Dr. Mathis's philosophy. He's condemned me to confinement until he returns in May, and if he doesn't think I'm better by then, I'll be sent to an asylum."

"An asylum? Is *he* mad?" Peter looked outraged. "When he returns, tell him you're cured. It's not a lie. There was nothing wrong with you in the first place."

"It's not so easy. If he thinks that his prescribed treatment is working, he may make it permanent."

"You mean, you'll be expected to stay locked up in this house? What better is that than an asylum? You're a prisoner either way." When Nathan dropped his eyes and said nothing, Peter softened and gave a playful smile. "I'll help you escape, if need be," he said. "Stow you away on the horse cart beneath tree trimmings and take you somewhere no one knows you. We'll live as fugitives."

Nathan grinned. "I'm afraid I don't possess many practical skills. How would I make it in the world?"

"I'll teach you what I know. And if you don't have a talent for horticulture, perhaps we can find work in the circus."

Nathan laughed. "Let's hope it doesn't come to that." It struck him then how tired he was, even after sleeping earlier in the day. Admittedly, it hadn't been very restful. He yawned.

"I should let you try to sleep. Besides, they might send out a search party for me if I'm not back soon. Mr. Millican expects me to report to him when I'm finished."

"Don't tell the others, please. About what I told you. I don't want them treating me differently."

"Of course." Peter smiled, "It was good talking with you."

"I thought so, too. In fact, this might be the most I've said to anyone since April began."

"If I have time, I'll stop by again tomorrow night, too. If you'd like."

"I'd like that very much," he said sleepily.

After Peter left, Nathan leaned back against his pillows and thought about Violet. Hers was a completely different mentality to the one Nathan had been raised with, and for that reason, part of him envied Peter's upbringing. Another, stronger part of him, though, was happy he had her for a mother. He took comfort in knowing that Peter wouldn't judge him for his oddities.

The room felt brighter in the lamplight than it did before, and the shadows bore no weight on Nathan's mind.

15

Peter visited Nathan every night after closing the house, and it became the highlight of his day. Mr. Millican, who had quickly gained confidence in Peter, stopped asking him to check in, so with no one to report to, Peter stayed with Nathan for close to an hour most nights, talking and laughing.

Peter told him about the progress he'd been making in the greenhouse and on the grounds. Nathan talked about the books he was reading and loaned one of his favorites to Peter to discuss once he finished. They took turns recounting amusing anecdotes and talked selectively about childhood memories. The conversation always ambled in warm, shallow waters, and that was fine by Nathan. Preferable, in fact. He didn't have the strength to explore darker depths in his current state. Something in him was mending, and Peter seemed to sense that, too.

He was beginning to sleep normally again. Talking with Peter before bed seemed to keep his night terrors at bay. As a result, he no longer slept through meals and was able to indulge his returning appetite. Steadily, he grew stronger in both body and mind. Every day felt better than the last.

The air around him tasted crisp and sweet. Rays of sunshine pouring in from the windows sang in splendid harmony. Healthy, pink roses bloomed on his cheeks.

Jude noticed the difference right away. "You're looking better," she said one morning. "I don't know what's changed, but I'm glad to see you out of bed and looking so well."

"I'm glad to be feeling better," Nathan said from his conservatory chair. She set out tea for him and turned to leave. "Jude, please stay for a moment. I'd like to apologize."

"Apologize? For what?"

He couldn't meet her eyes. "I've been unbearable lately. But you've been nothing but kind and concerned for me. I yelled at you when I had absolutely no right to. I wish I— If I could take it back…" He took a breath and looked up at her. "I'm just so sorry, Jude. You're my dearest friend."

She looked at him thoughtfully and said nothing—just studied his face. Finally, she said, "You know, when you were a boy, you had the rosiest cheeks. I thought you outgrew them." She placed a gentle hand on his face for a moment and smiled fondly. "Lunch will be soon. Any special requests for the cook?"

He smiled back and shook his head. "No. Thank you, Jude."

———

April was quickly drawing to a close, and Nathan had been purposefully avoiding any and all thoughts of Dr. Mathis. He knew it was senseless to pretend the doctor's return was anything but inevitable, but he feared that acknowledging the storm cloud on the horizon would pop his newfound buoyancy like a soap bubble. Dr. Mathis would be visiting the summer home next week, and until then, Nathan did not want to disturb his reverie with worry.

Despite his efforts, unexpected news broke Nathan's calm anyway. He received a letter from his mother one evening and opened it after dinner, thinking he would be treated to a lighthearted update on inconsequential family matters. Instead, the rug was pulled from beneath his feet. Again and again, he read the letter, looking frantically for any small scrap of hope, but he could find none. He crumpled to the floor.

Peter would be by soon, as usual, and Nathan was humiliated at the thought of being found like this, a blubbering mess on the carpet. He tried to compose himself, but there was no stopping his emotions.

The shadows in the corners of the room grew darker and heavier. Faint whispers echoed through his chambers. The wretched feeling of hopelessness brushed up against his ribs.

Then, there came a gentle knock at the door. A part of Nathan wanted more than anything to see Peter in that moment, but another part of him was too ashamed to be seen as he was. He thought about calling out that he wasn't feeling well tonight and that he wished to be alone, but he didn't trust his voice.

Without waiting for an answer, the door opened. It was Jude. They were equally surprised at the sight of the other.

"Nathan? My God, what's happened?" She made quick strides across the room and kneeled beside him.

He pathetically lifted the letter from his mother, "Daniel… He's getting married. The wedding will be held here at the summer home in August."

Her brows drew together in confusion. "Isn't that joyous news?"

Nathan let out a sob. "Don't you understand? There's nowhere near enough room in the London house for Daniel and his wife to start a family. Every Hambleton heir has raised their children in this house, and Daniel will be no different! Then what will become of me? Sent back to London to live with my mother and father? I'm not ready, Jude. What will happen when my father finds my presence unbearable and wishes to send me away again? I'll tell you. He'll have me sent to an asylum with Dr. Mathis's blessing! It doesn't matter what I say to the doctor next week, it won't be enough to thwart the inevitable. I may have three or four months at most before my freedom is taken from me."

Jude pursed her lips and gave him a cross look. "In all the years we've known each other, I've never known you to be so selfish and obtuse."

He was aghast. "*Selfish?*"

"Yes, *selfish,*" she repeated. "Your brother has found love and intends to start a family, but you can think only about yourself. How quick you are to find personal misery in someone else's happiness!" Nathan tried to speak but she continued. "And, frankly, you're mistaken if you think you'll find sympathy when discussing the subject of freedom with someone who has spent their life in domestic service. Every day you have the freedom to awaken when you feel fit, to dress as you want, to eat whatever you like. You can spend your day however you please. And before you remind me of Dr. Mathis's prescription, I wish to remind *you* that for the months prior to his decision, you voluntarily chose to lock yourself away from the world and live as a hermit. It's only now that you can't leave the house that you so desperately want to. Because you only appreciate the things you no longer have. And now, here you are bemoaning your loss, not realizing that, even now, you still have so much more than most."

Nathan sat in red-faced silence. He'd never been spoken to like this, by Jude or anyone. Guilt knotted itself in his stomach.

"I'm sorry," he said meekly. "You're right. I don't know what to say."

"Don't say anything. Just listen. There are people in this world that would have you believe you are utterly weak and yielding. That you have no say in the matters of your own happiness. Bollocks. You aren't a frail child. You never were. You've always been stronger than you've thought. You've just chosen to believe others who've told you otherwise."

"But Dr. Mathis—"

"Dr. Mathis is a bitter, old lemon unfit for the pig trough. And you'd do well to tell him as much!" She huffed and pushed a strand of fiery red hair out of her face. "Actually, you'd better not. But I meant what I said. He's a loathsome, louse of a man who values his own haughty opinions over the welfare of his patients."

Nathan watched Jude, flustered and agitated, smooth back her hair and attempt to compose herself. He'd never seen her so impassioned before. He couldn't help grinning.

"What? Why're you smiling?"

"A lemon unfit for the pig trough?" Unable to stop himself, he broke into a fit of giggles. Jude tried to remain serious, but soon she, too, dissolved into laughter. "I may never be able to look at him the same way."

She grinned. "I daresay you'll finally be seeing him as he really is. Now, as for this," she picked up the letter from Nathan's mother, "I understand why you're scared. But don't concede defeat before you've even tried. *You* might doubt yourself, but I've got my money on you."

"Thanks, Jude. Really. I needed to hear that. And I am sorry. You were right before; I was being insensitive."

"I know you didn't mean it," she gave his shoulder a small squeeze and then helped him to his feet. "I'm off to bed, but will you be all right? Do you need anything before I turn in?"

"No, thanks. I'll be fine. Wait— Why did you come here, anyway?"

"Oh, Peter asked me to. Today's his birthday, you know."

"*What?* It's his birthday?" Nathan racked his brain to recall if Peter had mentioned it before. He was certain that he hadn't, and a part of him felt disappointed by this.

"Yes. Mrs. Blake made him a cake, and I said I'd close the house for him. He asked me to check on you. I thought it was a strange request, but I told him I would." She looked at him expectantly for an explanation.

"Since he's started closing the house, he sits and talks with me in the evenings." He wasn't sure why he felt so bashful admitting it. "Maybe he thought I needed company in his absence." Jude looked rather pleased to hear this and gave him a knowing smile, which made him feel even more embarrassed.

"Well, you know, I'm sure he's still awake if you wanted to wish him a happy birthday before bed."

"Oh," he waved a hand as nonchalantly as he could. "Don't be preposterous. I'll just tell him tomorrow."

"All right, but if you change your mind, his room is at the end of the hall in the servants' quarters. On the left. Goodnight." And with that, she hurried out.

In the quiet of his chambers, Nathan debated whether he should go see Peter. It was possible he was in bed by now, and Nathan didn't want to bother him. But not seeing Peter on his birthday didn't sit well with him either.

—

Nathan knocked lightly. The hall was dark except for the thin sliver of yellow light glowing from beneath Peter's door. He heard a small shuffle on the other side and felt a flutter of anticipation.

Peter opened the door wearing his nightshirt. He looked both surprised and pleased to see him. "Nathan! What are you doing here?"

"I missed our usual evening conversation and wanted to say hello. Only for a moment. I won't keep you long, I promise."

"Nonsense. Please, come in." Peter ushered him into his room. It was a humble space with a small bed, a writing desk, a wardrobe, and a nightstand. On the bed lay the book Nathan had lent to him. "I was just reading your book, in fact."

They sat opposite each other, Peter on his bed and Nathan in the chair from the writing desk. It was tight quarters, but neither of them seemed to mind.

"Jude said that it was your birthday."

"That's right. Another year older."

"Why didn't you tell me?" Nathan stuck out his leg and playfully knocked it against Peter's.

"I wanted to," Peter explained. "I thought I would tell you tonight when I saw you, like always. But then, Mrs. Fairchild offered to close the house for me. And I know she was doing a nice thing, so I didn't want to tell her no.

That's why I asked her to check on you. I didn't want you thinking I'd closed the house without so much as a hello."

"I see," Nathan smiled. "You know, I'm rather glad you did. We ended up having an exceptional conversation. But, when I learned it was your birthday, I felt I had to see you and extend my felicitations."

Peter grinned from ear to ear. "I'm happy you did. It didn't feel right, not seeing you. My nighttime routine felt incomplete."

Nathan laughed, "As did mine. I think I can rest peacefully now." He rose to his feet. "True to my word, I won't bother you any longer. Especially not on your birthday. But I did want you to have this." From his pocket, Nathan retrieved the kaleidoscope he found with Peter in the greenhouse. It wasn't wrapped, but he did manage to find a small silk ribbon in his room that he tied into an unattractive bow.

"My goodness," Peter breathed, carefully taking it into his hands. "Nathan, I couldn't possibly accept this."

"Please, I'd like you to have it."

"But what about your brother? I thought you had plans to give him the biscuit tin?"

"I still do, but he won't know anything's missing. It was my kaleidoscope anyway. And besides, I really would like you to keep it. You'll forgive me for being sentimental, but our friendship has meant a great deal to me. It's given me a brighter and, dare I say, more colorful perspective. I wanted to provide the same for you and thought this would do the trick."

Peter laughed and pulled Nathan into an unexpected hug. All at once, Nathan was enveloped by Peter's scent—the sweet aroma of hay and freshly tilled earth. A smell that evoked warm, sunny days and lush, green pastures. It was intoxicating. Nathan felt his face instantly flush red and hot.

"Thank you," Peter said, pulling away and examining his gift. Nathan hoped the light in the room was too dim for Peter to see the color in his cheeks.

"You're quite welcome. And with that, I'll wish you goodnight."

"Of course," Peter said, still beaming. "Goodnight. I'll see you tomorrow."

"I'm looking forward to it."

Back in his room, as he settled into bed and tried to sleep, Nathan thought about Peter's embrace. Brief though it was, the sensation lingered with him. In his mind, Nathan still maintained that Jude was his dearest friend, but Peter was something else. Theirs was a friendship unlike any he'd known before. In that moment, he felt tremendously grateful for both of them.

Thoughts of Dr. Mathis came to him then, but he didn't cower from them. Instead, he felt a small fire burning within himself—a ferocity that was utterly unfamiliar to him. Jude was right. Dr. Mathis *was* a loathsome, louse of a man. And his words had held power over Nathan for long enough.

16

Dr. Mathis came the following Friday, and Nathan was ready. Upon his arrival, Jude brought the doctor to the study where Nathan sat at his writing desk, drafting a letter to his mother. He looked up as if surprised to see him.

"Oh, Dr. Mathis! How good to see you," he smiled. "That's all for now, Mrs. Fairchild. Thank you."

The doctor appeared agitated. "Your footman didn't take my bags to my room. Didn't you know I was coming? Or had you forgotten?"

"Ah, yes, I do apologize about that. I'm afraid we're in no position to accommodate guests at the moment." He casually folded his letter and put it into his breast pocket.

Dr. Mathis gaped. It was more emotion than Nathan had ever seen from him. "No position to—? I beg your pardon!"

"Yes, we're a bit shorthanded. I'm sure you've heard that our estate manager, Mr. Millican, took a rather nasty fall last month. But rest assured, I've arranged for you to stay at an inn in the village. Charming place. I'm sure you'll find it more than satisfactory. One of our chauffeurs will take you. In fact, the carriage should be outside now."

"Nathaniel, I did not come all this way to be sent to some cheap room in the local village!"

"Quite right. You came to check on my progress. Well, I'm pleased to tell you that your treatment worked. I'm cured. And really, I can't thank you enough."

"Cured?" Dr. Mathis was incredulous.

"Indeed. I considered telling you by post but thought it was best for you to see for yourself."

"See *what* for myself? You're not cured. That simply isn't possible."

"Not possible? I'm afraid I don't know what you mean."

"You've been sick your entire life, Nathaniel! I've been familiar with your condition since you were a boy, and I refuse to believe you've been cured by a few weeks of rest."

Nathan smiled, "You're being modest, doctor. You shouldn't underestimate the effectiveness of your methods."

"I am *not* underestimating my methods." Dr. Mathis was turning red in the face. "But I'm telling you, the treatment could not possibly have had such a dramatic effect!"

"Forgive me, but I was under the impression that you prescribed the treatment because you thought it would help me. Is that not true?"

"Well, yes, but—"

"And you said yourself that every doctor wishes to see their patients get better. I should think you'd be overjoyed to see me doing so well."

"I-I am, but—"

Nathan rose calmly from his desk, "And I daresay, you wouldn't want anyone to accuse you of lining your pockets by exaggerating the necessity for lengthy treatments and frequent visits."

"I beg your pardon!"

"I didn't think so. As such, I think we can both agree that my recovery could not be timelier. Truly a miracle on all counts."

Struggling to find words, Dr. Mathis opened and closed his mouth like a fish out of water. Nathan walked beside the doctor and put an arm around his shoulder, leading him to the hallway.

"Now, I'm afraid I must bring our conversation to an end, as I have business to attend to today. But I'm more than happy to walk you out."

Dr. Mathis shook off Nathan's arm and stomped his foot on the ground, *"Goddammit, stop this nonsense!"* His face was as red as a tomato. "I come all the way here from London, and you treat me with flagrant disrespect, dismissing me like I'm nobody of importance. Then, you make absurd claims about your health and *outrageous* accusations about my practices. Now, I don't know who you think you're speaking with, but I will not tolerate this. I am your *doctor,* and you will do as *I* say!"

Nathan remained unshaken. "Dr. Mathis, I understand you may be disappointed about the changes to your sleeping arrangement, but I'm surprised to see you so upset. It's a minor inconvenience at best, but evidently, it's proven to be too much excitement for you. Perhaps a few weeks of bed rest will help you with your stress. It proved effective for me, and I feel certain it would for you also."

Hands balled into tight fists, Dr. Mathis glared at him with white-hot fury in his eyes. "You can pretend all you like that you're cured, but I know your brother's getting married, Nathaniel. And when he does, you'll be forced back to London, and you won't be able to hide yourself from your father. When he sees you for the lunatic you are, he'll have you committed. And I will do everything in my power to ensure you are never released."

Nathan met Dr. Mathis's eyes with a long and level stare. "Your carriage awaits you, doctor. Do try to enjoy your stay at the inn."

With gritted teeth the doctor turned on his heel and marched down the hallway. Once around the corner and out of sight, Nathan released a tremulous breath. Not a moment later, Jude appeared as if from nowhere.

"How'd it go?"

"Don't act like you weren't listening," he smirked.

She grinned. "You were great. I mean it, you really were. I doubt if that old bastard has ever had the tables turned on him like that before. I only wish I could've seen his face."

"I must admit, I feel fantastic. I know it isn't over, of course. I'll have to figure out a way to face my father when the time comes, but that's a problem for another day."

"I couldn't agree more. You deserve to celebrate this victory, and on such a beautiful day I might add."

"Is everything ready?"

"Yes. Take the path behind the barn to the trees."

"Thanks, Jude." He kissed her on the cheek and all but ran out of the house into the brilliant May sunshine.

17

Outside, Nathan paused to take in the day. The world around him was green and bright and warm. He relished the sun on his face and felt the ice of winter that clung to his bones finally begin to thaw.

It was late morning, Dr. Mathis was gone, and Nathan had the entire day ahead of him. Possibility was palpable in the air.

With a spring in his step, he took the walkway around to the rear of the house. Just past the barn, a thin footpath worn into the earth branched off from the main walkway and led toward the treeline that surrounded the property. He took the path per Jude's direction and felt a fluttering sense of anticipation.

At the edge of the estate, trees grew in a dense line, the space between them filled by a hedgerow, but there was a small break in the perimeter. He passed through the gap and found Peter leaning against a tree, waiting for him on the other side. Peter looked recently shaved and wore a comfortable looking white buttoned shirt with the sleeves rolled to his elbows. His strong forearms were folded casually across his chest. Seeing Peter, Nathan found that words suddenly escaped him. They stared at each other for a moment, not saying anything.

"Well?" Peter asked expectantly, breaking the silence.

"I don't think Dr. Mathis will be back," Nathan said, unable to stop himself smiling.

Peter exploded with joy, shaking a victorious fist in the air, "That's fantastic!" He looked at Nathan with pride and pulled him into an embrace. This time Nathan was ready, and he hugged him back in earnest. When Peter pulled away, he was grinning still and seemed unaware that he was still holding onto Nathan's arms. Their faces were still very close, and Nathan pinked. "Are you ready?"

"Utterly," Nathan said. "Lead the way."

Peter picked up the picnic basket by his feet. Jude had arranged the basket and orchestrated for Peter to have the day off from working the grounds. She'd told Mr. Millican that Nathan planned to survey the full extent of the property to see if the land could be put to better use and, as such, needed a guide to accompany him.

"I've got a spot in mind," Peter said. "Let's be off."

Nathan followed him away from the summer home. With every step, his body felt lighter; with every breath, his mind felt clearer. They walked through open, green pastures and over gently rolling hills. Pillowy, white clouds passed leisurely overhead.

Nathan noticed that Peter was watching him amusedly. "What's that look for?"

"You were humming that song again," Peter said. "The same one from the greenhouse. It's lovely whatever it is."

"Was I? I hadn't noticed." Feeling bashful, he changed the subject, "We've been walking for a while. Are we nearly there?"

"You're not getting tired already, are you?"

"Tired? No. Hungry? That's a different matter."

"Hold on for a bit longer. It'll be worth it."

Peter led him up a particularly large hill. The climb was the most notable physical activity Nathan had experienced in many months. Halfway up, he had unbuttoned his waistcoat and rolled his sleeves like Peter's. He was breathless, his legs burned, and he felt thoroughly invigorated.

When they finally reached the top, they were treated to a spectacular, sprawling view of the countryside. Crop fields laid next to each other like patchwork, vast herds of sheep grazed in pastures, farmhouses dotted the landscape sparingly. All at once, the world seemed much bigger than Nathan remembered. For nearly seven months, life had been contained within the walls of the summer home. Seeing the world now, from this vantage, was a revelation.

"My God," he said to himself.

"I told you it'd be worth it," Peter grinned. "It's a perfect spot for a picnic."

Standing with them at the top of the hill was a large, lone maple. They laid the linen sheet Jude packed for them in the shade of the tree and set out their lunch. Fresh bread, cheeses, cured sausage, and gherkins. She'd also included a bottle of ginger beer for them to share.

"How did you find this place?" Nathan asked around a mouthful of bread. His family would be appalled by his conduct, but he hardly cared. Peter didn't seem to mind and that mattered more to him.

"I found it my first month here actually. On a day off. Mr. Millican told me your family owns a fair bit of the land surrounding the estate and that your father allows the pastures to be used for grazing." He shrugged, "I decided to explore a bit. I'm glad I did."

"Do you typically go exploring on your days off?"

"Usually. I much prefer it out here than in the village."

"Why's that?"

Peter took a sip of ginger beer and then passed the bottle to Nathan. "Well, there isn't much to do in the village that doesn't involve spending money."

"Are you saving for something?" He cut off two slices of sausage and handed one of them to Peter.

"No, not anymore." A wounded look flashed across his face. "But I do send as much as I can to my parents."

The shadows on and around Peter seemed suddenly dense and heavy. There was something clearly weighing on him. Nathan studied his face for a moment, before sitting up and dusting the crumbs from his hands.

"You know," he began, "Believe it or not, you know a great deal more about me than most anyone else. However, I feel that there is still so much I don't know about you. I'm beginning to feel it isn't quite fair."

Peter smiled despite himself. "I thought you knew things about people without needing to be told."

Nathan laughed, "Well, aren't you cheeky?" They hadn't spoken about his condition since that first night Peter closed the house, but it was remarkable to Nathan how easy it felt to be talking about it now in casual conversation. He was happy he confided in Peter. It made him feel less alone.

"Perhaps," Peter grinned. "Do I really know you better than most people? What about Mrs. Fairchild?"

"You're avoiding the subject."

He sighed, "Yes, I suppose you're right. I haven't been fair. It isn't that I don't trust you. It's that I'm— I know I shouldn't, but I feel so…"

Nathan caught a word like a whisper on the wind. "Ashamed."

Peter looked surprised for a moment, then smiled ruefully. "That's right."

"What *really* brought you here?" Nathan asked cautiously.

Peter looked at his hands and took a deep breath. "I was running away."

"From what?"

"From whom, more like." He cleared his throat. "I left home for London because I was in love. Her name was Sarah."

Something bitter and cold constricted in Nathan's chest like a snake. The sensation took him off guard—it felt strangely like jealousy. He quickly pushed the thought away and didn't let on to Peter.

"We'd known each other a long time. About ten years ago, after her father died, she moved to my village with her younger brother to live with their aunt. Over time, we fell in love, and I had plans of marrying her and taking over my father's farm.

"But their aunt was an old woman, and about a year ago she passed suddenly in her sleep. After that, Sarah went to London to find work for herself. I couldn't stand to be apart, so I followed her. I lived with family friends and took a job to save up money for our wedding."

"I don't understand. You have your father's farm. Surely that should provide enough to marry. Why didn't you propose to her before she left for the city?"

"Well, it isn't just about Sarah. Her brother, Andrew... He lost an arm in the same accident that took their father. They worked together in the mines. One day the roof collapsed, and six men lost their lives. Andrew was lucky to survive, but of course, his injury left him with no job prospects. He's a young man now, but he can't provide for himself. When their aunt passed, Sarah struggled to take care of both herself and Andrew, and that's why she went to the city looking for better work.

"For her, marriage isn't only about her own future but also her brother's. I had to prove to her that I could provide for them both. That's why I took a job in London. It paid well, and I planned to spend a year or two saving every penny I could to show her that I was more than capable. After that, I imagined that the three of us would return to the farm, I'd take the reins from my father, and we'd begin our life together."

Nathan watched Peter. His eyes were fixed on something far away as if no longer at the picnic at all.

"What happened?" Nathan asked softly.

Peter sighed. "Something I should mention about Sarah is that she's exceedingly beautiful, albeit very humble about her appearance. In London, another man took a fancy to her. A man of nobility. And wealth. She called off our informal engagement, saying it was the sensible thing to do."

"*Sensible?* I can't imagine anything *less* sensible than throwing away the chance to spend a life with you," Nathan said with more feeling than he intended. That anyone could leave someone like Peter for the sake of money was beyond his comprehension.

Peter's cheeks turned rosy, and he looked away. Nathan only then realized how his statement sounded.

"I-I mean what a horrible thing," he quickly tried to explain, "to sacrifice love and happiness for money. You would've made an exceptional husband and father."

"That's kind of you to say," Peter said with a small smile. "But, from Sarah's perspective, it was an opportunity to give Andrew a life without worry. Money would never be a concern."

"I'm sorry. I really am," Nathan said solemnly, and he meant it. While he detested the thought of Peter being with someone like Sarah, he saw the hurt in his eyes. "But why come here? Why not go back home?"

"I was supposed to return home with Sarah and the promise of starting a family. To go back alone means I've truly given up on the life I imagined for myself. I guess that's something that I'm not ready to do just yet. I need time to mourn that dream before returning. But I couldn't stay in London. So, I found myself here instead."

"What do your parents think of you being here?"

Peter tugged at the hem of his trousers. "They don't know I am. I send money with my previous London residence as the return address."

"You mean, they have no idea you're not still in London?" Nathan was shocked.

"Oh, I'm sure they know by now. When I got the position here, rather than admit the truth, I told our family friends that I was going back home. They've almost certainly received letters from my parents addressed to me since I've left and realized what I've done—that I lied to them. I know my parents must be concerned, but so long as I'm sending them money, they know I'm alright."

"I don't understand why you didn't tell them."

Suddenly, Peter's eyes welled up with tears, and he lowered his head. "Because I'm a coward, that's why." He let out a strangled sob.

Alarmed, Nathan quickly moved beside him and put an arm around his shoulder. "Oh, Peter! Don't say something so horrible."

"But it's true," he croaked. "My parents both need me home. I know I should go back. Here I sit, enjoying the day as if everything is fine, but it isn't. I've run away from the problems in my life like a child." Peter buried his face into his hands and shook softly as he cried.

"Well, I'm glad you did," Nathan said finally.

Peter looked up at him, brows pinched together in confusion. His eyes were swollen and wet, his cheeks florid and hot. In that moment, Nathan felt an overwhelming urge to cradle Peter's face in his hands and brush away the tears with his thumbs.

"I'm being serious," he continued. "I can't bear to think where I'd be this very moment if we hadn't met. You've helped me maintain my sanity over this year. There was such darkness at times, I wasn't sure I would live to see another day, but I'm here now because of you. And it's so much more than merely surviving. I can't remember the last time I felt so *strong*. Need I remind you that I stood up to Dr. Mathis today for the first time in my life?"

"You give me too much credit," Peter said modestly, wiping his eyes.

"On the contrary, you don't give yourself enough. Perhaps, what you assumed was a selfish reason for coming here was really an intuition."

Peter gave a wet laugh. "You sound like my mother."

"I shall take that as a compliment. Ever since you told me of your mother, I've aspired to be more like her. Learning that she also lives with gifts like mine has given me greater hope than anything else. For the first time, I feel I have a future ahead of me that doesn't involve an institution."

A smile brightened Peter's face for a moment before a thought dawned in his eyes and he became somber again. "She's not doing well, my mother. She's become forgetful these past few years which is very unlike her. It started off small, but now, she sometimes forgets important things like where she is or who she's speaking with. The last letter I received from my father while I was in London said she's gotten worse. I know he needs me there. They both do..." He sighed and ran a frustrated hand through his hair. "God, it's all gone so wrong. I left for the city with visions of marriage and beginning a family. Now, Sarah's gone, and I'm slowly losing my mother."

Nathan hugged him tighter. "You're not a coward, Peter. In fact, I think it takes a great deal of courage to admit when you can't handle something. That's not to say you never will. You may simply need more time. Don't berate yourself for merely being human."

Peter looked up at him and a small smile tugged at the corners of his mouth. "You're a wonder. Thank you." He let his head fall to the base of Nathan's neck and exhaled a sigh. Nathan felt the tension in Peter's body soften.

18

After packing away lunch, Peter and Nathan laid next to each other on the sheet and watched the clouds. Nathan discovered that Peter had a truly remarkable imagination and could see the likeness of something in nearly any shape.

"What about that one?" Nathan pointed.

"A horse-drawn carriage."

"You're lying! I don't see that at all."

"Look there," he gestured upwards. "That's the head of one of the horses. And that there— That's the coachman. Do you see? It's not a carriage in profile. Rather, it's coming towards us."

Suddenly, Nathan could see the scene perfectly as if looking at a photograph. "By God, I see it now. You've really got quite an eye for this."

Since their conversation over lunch, the air between them had become different. From the very beginning, many months ago, they'd quickly found comfort and easiness with each other, but now, it was markedly more pronounced. The last plates of armor between them had fallen away, and what remained was an openness and wholeness unlike anything Nathan had ever known.

Peter rolled onto his side and propped himself on an elbow. "Well, what about you?" he teased. "You have an eye for things I can't even perceive. Tell me, what sorts of things can you see at this very moment?"

"Well, I see a rather dapper mug with bold features and kind eyes."

"Do be serious," Peter feigned exasperation.

"If I'm honest, I make quite an effort to *not* see things that aren't there," Nathan admitted.

"Would you try?"

He studied Peter for a moment—his face was as eager as a child's. It made him smile, and his doubts quickly melted.

"Oh, all right." Nathan propped himself up and looked out at the view over the countryside. Peter beamed.

At first, Nathan felt awkward. He'd never attempted this before. The visions and whispers he experienced came to him like ghosts, choosing to appear of their own volition. He wasn't confident he could conjure anything through his own effort. Still, he tried.

He quieted his thoughts as best he could and let his eyes roam freely, trusting that they would lead him to something. At first, he saw nothing out of the ordinary. The day around them was still bright and golden. Then suddenly, on the horizon, a dark blanket of purple clouds appeared across the sky. At that moment, a gentle breeze blew over the hill, but in the sound of the rustling grass Nathan heard a frenetic murmuring.

Rain.

"Anything?" Peter asked.

"Yes, actually," Nathan smiled. He felt an odd sense of accomplishment. "There's rain coming. A storm."

"Today?" Peter squinted up at the calm sky overhead.

"That's right. In fact, I think we should make our way back now. I get the sense it's moving quickly."

They packed up their picnic and began the trek back to the summer home. Nathan was sad to be leaving their place on the hill. He was already thinking of ways that he could steal Peter away from the estate for another outing without being too obvious. He didn't want the rest of the staff to think that Peter was receiving special preference, even if he was.

Halfway back, the weather began to change. The wind picked up, and the sky grew dark with ominous clouds. Thunder rumbled in the distance.

Peter flashed Nathan a knowing grin. "I never doubted you for a second," he said over the howl of the wind.

As they approached the summer home's surrounding treeline, heavy drops of rain began to fall on their heads. Peter held the picnic basket close to his chest and began to run, calling out to Nathan over his shoulder to follow his lead. They cut through the gap in the hedgerow and ran towards the barn.

By the time they made it into the dry sanctuary of the stables, the rain had begun to pour and soaked their shirts and hair. They looked at each other, panting, and broke out into laughter.

"Didn't quite make it to the house, but it could've been worse I suppose," Nathan said, looking around the barn.

Peter called out to see if anyone was there besides them and the horses. They were alone. At this realization, a playful glint flashed in his eyes.

"Follow me."

Nathan followed him to a wooden ladder that led up to an opening in the ceiling. He climbed up behind Peter and found himself in the hayloft. The sweet, earthy scent of hay surrounded them completely, and the drone of the rain sounded particularly loud in the rafters.

"It doesn't matter how old I get, I always feel like a child in haylofts," Peter smiled. He set down the picnic basket and retrieved the sheet. It was still dry. He laid it out on a shallow bed of hay and then began unbuttoning his shirt.

"What are you doing?" Nathan asked, alarmed.

"I'm not waiting for the rain to pass in wet clothes," he said matter-of-factly. "You better do the same. If you come down with another fever, Mrs. Fairchild will have my head." He stripped off his shirt and draped it over one of the attic beams to dry. Then, starting at the base of his throat, he unbuttoned his undergarments down to his waist and peeled them back revealing his arms and chest.

Nathan caught himself staring and quickly turned away to unbutton his own shirt. He felt immensely self-conscious of his own body all of a sudden. He stripped off his vest and shirt but kept his undergarments on.

Peter was lying on the makeshift hay bed with hands resting easily on his stomach. He looked over at Nathan and patted the space beside him. It was a small blessing, Nathan thought, that their trousers hadn't gotten damp as well. When he settled onto the sheet, Peter reached over and pinched a piece of his undershirt between his thumb and forefinger.

"Are you dry enough?"

"I'm quite all right," Nathan assured. "Thank you."

They laid together and listened to the sound of the rain. Nathan's self-consciousness from before was now miles away. Laying here with Peter, listening to the steady drumming of raindrops and occasional roll of thunder, felt as natural as anything.

"I did this when I was a kid sometimes," Peter said softly. "On rainy days when there's nothing to be done in the fields, I would hide away in the hayloft and just listen like we are now. Sometimes I'd doze off. It was always the best sleep."

Nathan hummed thoughtfully. He could imagine a young Peter sleeping in a large pile of hay. Feeling drowsy now himself, the thought of a nap was very appealing.

"Peter, can I ask you something? I hope it won't upset you."

"Nonsense. Ask anything you'd like."

"It's a thought I had when you were talking at lunch," he said. "What is it like to be in love?"

Peter rolled onto his side to face Nathan. "You mean, you've never been in love before?"

Nathan studied the ceiling. "I can't say I have. I've found people beautiful before, but it is a fleeting thought. Never what I imagined love to be like. I've begun to worry in recent years that I'm simply incapable."

"I very much doubt that." There was a conviction in Peter's voice that made Nathan feel suddenly close to tears.

"Do you mean it?" Nathan said, swallowing back the tightness in his throat.

"Absolutely. I believe it's simply a matter of not having met the right person."

"Now, you're starting to sound like *my* mother," Nathan chuckled. "But how will I know? What does it feel like?" He rolled on his side to face Peter now.

"Well, I'm not sure what I can say about it that hasn't already been said by countless poets throughout history," Peter grinned, "but it's something that happens without any effort at all. It's like finding a piece of yourself in another person that you didn't realize was missing. It's the happiest you've ever been but also the most frightened. It's realizing your heart is made of the most delicate porcelain and then giving it to someone else for safe keeping."

Nathan was suddenly aware how small the space was between them. He opened his mouth to say something, but the thought dissolved as he stared into the calm blue of Peter's eyes. They sang a song of carefree conversations and easy afternoons. Nathan's pulse stuttered, and he felt lightheaded as if dreaming.

Peter placed a hand on Nathan's shoulder and smiled reassuringly, though his eyes betrayed a small sliver of sadness. "You'll know when it happens." Then, he rolled onto his back and stared at the ceiling again. "Mrs. Fairchild must be worried sick about you. If this rain doesn't let up soon, I'm afraid she might send out a search party."

"Let's hope not," Nathan said absently, rolling onto his back.

"I might shut my eyes for a bit," Peter yawned. He nestled into the hay and shifted closer to Nathan, their shoulders pressed together. In a matter of minutes, the rhythm of his breath became deep and slow as he slipped into sleep.

Nathan laid awake, staring at the rafters and very aware of Peter's arm, strong and warm against his. Deep within his chest, he felt an almost unbearable desire to be closer to Peter, to bury his face into the heat of his neck and join him in sleep. Instead, he remained as still as a statue, terrified.

You'll know when it happens.

Nathan pushed the thought from his mind fast and swore to himself that he'd never entertain such a laughable notion again. Peter was a friend—a great friend—and nothing more. A lack of meaningful friendships in his life has led him to misinterpret his own emotions, he reasoned. That is all.

He closed his eyes and let the sound of the rain drown his doubts.

19

Dear Nathaniel,

We received a rather alarming visit from Dr. Mathis today. He said that he had been by to see you for your health and that you behaved appallingly. I've never seen the doctor in such an emotional frenzy. In fact, I'm not sure I completely followed the ramblings of his diatribe. Regardless, I assured him I would speak with you on the matter (as if I have nothing better to do!).

As urgent as I'm sure the doctor imagines the situation to be, I frankly have more important things to tend to. I'm sure you've gleaned from my past letters that I am not particularly fond of Daniel's choice of fiancée. I have been trying to reason with him. I've all but begged him to stay in London through the entirety of The Season so that he may see firsthand how many beautiful and respectable women are still eligible for marriage. But it seems my motherly concern has only brought out the worst in his stubbornness, and now he has chosen to move the wedding from August to July out of spite.

Please, Nathaniel, can I trust that you will properly care for yourself and the summer home for the next two months before we get there? I will speak with you in person regarding the Dr. Mathis incident. Until then, I will be doing everything in my power to save your brother from his own stupidity.

All my love,

Mother

The news of Daniel's rapidly approaching nuptials sent waves through the summer home. While it wasn't clear whether the wedding plans would survive the meddling of Lady Hambleton, the staff bustled in preparation for the ceremony regardless. The house was thoroughly cleaned from top to bottom—floors waxed, chandeliers dusted, rugs and sofas beaten, silverware polished.

Outside, the grounds were also being readied. Now that the weather was warm and grass grew eagerly, seasonal mowers had been hired to help tend the lawn. Peter found himself very busy with landscaping projects and managing the new hires in Mr. Millican's absence. He pruned trees, shaped shrubs, and planted dazzling flowerbeds.

Nathan spent most of his time keeping out of everybody's way. He sat by the lake, down past the barn and beyond the gardens, under the shade of a tree and read. From there, he could easily see Peter who would come to sit with him every so often when he needed a break from the sun. Nathan would shuttle pitchers of lemonade, a rare treat for most laborers, out to the men working on the grounds and would attempt to volunteer his help. The idea of asking Lord Hambleton's son to assist with manual work was clearly an objectionable one, and his offers were politely declined. Peter, however, recruited Nathan's help with the flowerbeds. He taught him the names of the different flowers and showed him how to properly transplant them to the soil.

The greenhouse had transformed since Peter and Nathan had gone digging for treasure. There was an impressive collection of exotic plants and flowers of varying size and color. Per Nathan's request many months ago, Peter had included violets throughout the greenhouse, and they were now in full bloom. He'd planted strawberries as well which were beginning to flower and should produce fruit in a month's time. To his surprise, Nathan found that he enjoyed working with plants and soil, so he took it upon himself to look after the greenhouse—under Peter's guidance, of course. Many of the plants inside had very particular watering and pruning needs which Nathan conscientiously memorized and obliged. After a couple weeks, Peter joked that he would soon be out of a job at the rate Nathan was learning the trade.

"Does that make me your apprentice then?"

"Absolutely," Peter grinned. "And as such, Master Nathan, you should address me as Master Peter from now on."

—

Mr. Millican was beginning to show signs of improvement, but his wrist was still too weak to use crutches. Peter continued to close the house in the evenings on his behalf and, as always, stopped by to chat with Nathan.

"Why doesn't she like your brother's fiancée?" Peter asked him one night.

"Who knows with her. My mother is such a wonderfully kind woman, but she also has a rather unlikely tendency to be critical of inconsequential things. She says that she's trying to get Daniel to fully consider all of his options, but I'd wager that she would find fault in whomever he took a fancy to."

"Sounds like she's being protective."

"I think so. But she can't treat us as if we were children forever."

"Is it true that your brother will inherit this house when he marries?" Peter asked, taking a sudden interest in his fingernails.

"That's right."

"Does that mean you'll be leaving?"

"Yes, back to London." Nathan picked at a bit of fluff on his trousers. A loud silence stretched between them.

"I'll—" Peter stopped and seemed to debate his words. Then he looked up and flashed a halfhearted smile, "I suppose we'll have to make the most of the next couple months then. Maybe have another picnic if there's time."

"I'd really like that," Nathan said as brightly as he could.

Peter left for the night, and Nathan lied awake thinking about the day he will inevitably return to London. He imagined saying goodbye to Jude and Peter, his two greatest friends in the world, and watching them become smaller from the window of a carriage. A weight like a stone settled onto his chest. The thought was too much to bear. He rolled onto his side, buried his face into the pillow, and lost himself in a memory—laying next to Peter in the hayloft and listening to the rain.

———

"I can't believe how quickly we managed to do everything," Jude said, sipping her tea. "I thought we'd be working up to the last minute."

It was mid-June now and the manor was mostly ready for the bride and groom. For the first time in weeks, the staff had a chance to slow down and breathe.

"I know it'll be madness again in July when they arrive," she continued. "But I can't tell you how nice it is to have a moment's peace."

Nathan looked out of the conservatory windows at the grounds and admired all that had been accomplished. To say he played a minor role in the efforts was an overstatement, but still he felt a small sense of pride. He was eager to show the greenhouse to his mother and tell her about the different plants he'd been caring for.

"I'm going to miss this place," he said quietly. "It's funny, isn't it? Not two months ago, I desperately wanted to escape, and now I want to stay."

She looked at him with a sad smile. "I'll miss having you. And I know I'm not the only one. But it won't be forever, though, will it? After all, there's always the Hambleton Summer Holiday to look forward to."

Nathan turned his gaze back outside, "Can I ask you something?"

"Of course."

"I'm sure you recall our conversation from before, when I first learned about the wedding. Firstly, I want to thank you again for setting me right. As uncertain as I still am about what lies ahead of me, I am truly happy for Daniel.

"However, that night you also spoke of freedom. The freedom to live one's life as they wish. It's something I've been thinking about a great deal as of late, and I wanted to ask—What would it be like for you? To live freely?"

She seemed to consider this over another sip of tea. "For me, freedom is a home I can call my own. Every day I oversee this place, but none of it belongs to me. This house moves to the rhythm of someone else's schedule, and I simply uphold it. Freedom is eating when you'd like, cleaning when you'd like, opening the windows when you'd like." She set her cup in its saucer. "I had that once. With John. I was happier than I'd ever been. I remember thinking how lucky I was. I'd found the love of my life, and I finally had a home, a sanctuary. But, of course, I wasn't as lucky as I thought myself to be."

The bags beneath her eyes suddenly seemed heavier. Upon her face, Nathan saw a hopelessness he knew well from his own experience.

"There's still hope to have a home one day."

She said nothing, only smiled and shook her head softly. He didn't know what else he could say. He wanted to tell her with every certainty that she would find her freedom in time, but he didn't feel certain of anything. The future of his own happiness hung in the air like an unanswered question.

He turned back to the grounds and let his eyes move as they wished. Since the picnic, Nathan had tried not to shy away from his visions and, in fact, practiced voluntarily opening his mind to them. Now, as his eyes roamed, he hoped to glean some sort of insight for things to come, any small assurance that the road ahead would lead them to their hearts' desires.

A sudden and sharp pain struck him deep within his head, and he dropped his teacup onto his lap. The world swam around him, and an overwhelming feeling of inevitability pervaded his senses. Impending change loomed over him.

No sooner had the sensation overcome him than it disappeared entirely.

"Nathan? Are you all right?" Jude looked at him anxiously.

"Yes, but—"

Footsteps rapidly approached the conservatory and they both turned. It was Emily, pale and winded.

"It's Mr. Millican. He isn't waking."

20

"Apoplexy," Dr. Beverley said gravely. "It was likely the thing that made him fall in the first place, back in April, but it can be hard to identify when the patient doesn't remember the episode occurring. Which isn't uncommon."

Nathan looked down to a small and frail-looking Mr. Millican lying in his bed. "What can be done?"

"Not much I'm afraid. Those suffering from apoplexy may become comatose as Mr. Millican has, but the prognosis in these instances isn't clear. Some wake in a matter of days. Some weeks. Others don't wake at all."

"Weeks?" Jude asked. "How can anyone survive like this for weeks? Can he eat and drink in his current state?"

"Not on his own, and that is, unfortunately, my greatest concern," the doctor sighed. "A patient like this should be admitted to hospital. There, he would receive proper care and be given regular nutritive enemata to fulfill his dietary needs. However, considering Mr. Millican's age and physical state, the simple process of relocating him could prove fatal."

"What do you suggest we do?" Nathan asked.

Dr. Beverley delicately put his stethoscope back into his bag and closed it shut. He spoke gently, "I aspire to find hope wherever I am able. Few things in life are, in fact, hopeless. There is certainly still a chance that he will awaken in a day or two. However, I must be honest, the likelihood of Mr. Millican's recovery is poor. The most we can do in the meantime is ensure that he is comfortable and pray."

Jude and Nathan discussed whether they should notify his mother and father regarding Mr. Millican's health. They ultimately decided to wait. Nathan knew his mother was likely preoccupied with the impending wedding. It was senseless to create unnecessary worry for her. After all, albeit slim, there was still a chance Mr. Millican would wake.

As such, they took it upon themselves to care for the old man—cleaning him, adjusting his pillows, accompanying him at all hours. When it was Nathan's turn to sit with him, he found himself thinking back on a lifetime of memories he had with the estate manager. Mr. Millican had been the one who taught Nathan how to fasten a fishhook to his line when he was a boy, attempting to fish in the lake. And once when he was nine, Nathan had been stung by a wasp, and Mr. Millican carried him to the barn, tore open one of his cigarettes, and placed tobacco on the sting to stop the pain. He remembered digging for treasure in the greenhouse with Daniel, ruining the flowerbeds, and Mr. Millican halfheartedly scolding them, trying hard not to smile. Seeing the old man in his bed now, unresponsive and declining, deeply upset him. But work needed to be done, and he found strength with Jude to carry on.

Two days of little sleep and no improvement passed. With every hour, the residents of the manor felt less confident in Mr. Millican's recovery. In the afternoon, Jude relieved Nathan from his post and told him to get some rest. He considered going to his chambers and sleeping, but a desire to see Peter was stronger. He exited out the back of the house by way of the servants' entrance and found him in the greenhouse.

"How is he?" Peter asked.

"The same," Nathan said, scrubbing a hand over his face. "Which I suppose means, in actuality, he's doing worse. Every day is another without food or water. He can't go on like this much longer."

"What about you? Have you been eating? Or sleeping for that matter? You look exhausted."

"Some sleep. As for food, I had breakfast this morning. Although, that may have been yesterday now that I think about it."

"Well, there aren't many yet, but the first ripe strawberries of the season are ready. I was going to bring them to you and Jude to brighten your spirits, but since you're here now," he held out a small basket of succulent, ruby-colored strawberries.

Nathan's stomach grumbled, and he reached for the largest one he saw. "Thank you," he said gratefully and bit into the fruit. The flesh was firm but tender, juicy and sweet. He almost laughed at how delicious it was. "My God, these are divine."

Peter beamed and sat with Nathan on a nearby bench as he ate several more. Fatigue catching up to him, Nathan leaned against Peter and let his head fall to his shoulder. His eyes fluttered shut, and he felt very close to sleep.

Peter turned towards him and spoke softly, his lips brushing lightly against Nathan's hair, "You should go get some rest."

Nathan hummed thoughtfully in agreement but didn't move. The warmth of the greenhouse and physical comfort of Peter was too appealing to leave. His thoughts ambled and shifted lazily, quickly becoming less coherent. The taste of strawberries lingering on tongue brought him to an unfamiliar memory of Mr. Millican. The estate manager was a young boy standing beside his mother in their rural family home, pleading with her for a strawberry. Just one. *Please.* He knew they were meant for the market, but would one really matter? She handed him one, told him crossly not to tell his father, and shooed him away. Her arms were folded sternly, but she watched him go with a smile. It was the sweetest thing he'd ever tasted.

The foreign memory stirred Nathan from the edge of sleep and suddenly a realization surged through his body like an electric current. He sat upright, alert. Peter started.

"It's happening now," Nathan said and bolted from the greenhouse, Peter on his heels. They ran as quickly as they could across the lawn, through the servants' quarters, and into Mr. Millican's room. Jude was already on her feet and moving toward the door when they entered.

"I was just about to fetch you," she said urgently. "Come quick. His breathing has changed."

"It's started. He's dying." Nathan perched himself on the side of Mr. Millican's bed and looked at the old man's gaunt face, his skin pallid and thin.

"Should I send for Dr. Beverley?" Jude asked.

"Send the stableman, but I fear he will be gone before the doctor arrives. For the time being, all we can do is accompany him."

Jude sought out the stableman and returned in a matter of minutes. She stood with Peter a small distance away. They both seemed too anxious to sit. The room was heavy with the sound of Mr. Millican's wheezing breaths.

Unsure of what else to do, Nathan tentatively took one of the old man's hands into his own, and as he did, the world around him unexpectedly changed. No longer in the summer home, all he could see was golden light, surrounding him from every direction. He was no longer aware of his own body. He felt only a deep and comforting warmth that assuaged every worry he'd ever had over the course of his life. To Jude and Peter, Nathan's eyes appeared wide and distant, welling with tears.

"I can see him," Nathan told them, as figures emerged from the otherworldly glow around him. "He's a boy. So young and full of life. There isn't any pain at all. Just joy. My God, the joy." It radiated from every fiber of the young Mr. Millican that Nathan saw before him and coursed through his own body. He'd never felt anything like it. The boy ran by, unaware of Nathan, and threw his arms around a young girl. Mr. Millican's thoughts were becoming Nathan's own, and he suddenly knew who she was, witnessing in an instant every fond memory Mr. Millican had shared with her. "Oh, his sister! She's here!

They look so much alike. Lorna, it's been too long. Bless my soul, you look the same as when we were children."

"Nathan…" Jude said cautiously. But he could neither see nor hear her.

"Mother! Father!" Nathan laughed and tears spilled. "You're all here! I've missed you all so terribly. I can't believe you're here." He was overwhelmed with emotions—Mr. Millican's emotions—and they poured out of him freely. Nothing else in the world mattered besides the all-embracing warmth and golden light. It was pure, unending love.

Far away, in the summer home, Mr. Millican's breath thinned and slowed, unbeknownst to Nathan. Jude and Peter exchanged worried glances, uncertain if they should rouse Nathan from his trancelike state.

"We're almost home," Nathan laughed, fully sobbing now. "We're almost home."

Mr. Millican breathed his final breath, and all at once, Nathan was back in the room with Jude and Peter, and everything was as it was. He was immediately overcome with an emptiness within him. The warmth and light were gone. The joy of seeing long-lost loved ones, the tremendous love that moved through him—all gone. The world around him lacked color. Shivers overtook him as if he'd been submerged in ice water. His tears grew cold on his cheeks.

He turned to face Peter and Jude. They watched him intently. Nathan opened his mouth helplessly, trembling, but no words would come. Instead, he rose to his feet and quickly left the room, avoiding their eyes. Fresh tears threatened to fall.

In his chambers, he fell onto his bed and sobbed. The feeling in his chest, hollow and bleak, ached so immensely he was convinced he would never know happiness again. The world would forever pale in comparison to the sheer magnitude of joy he'd experienced only moments ago.

Then, Nathan heard his bedroom door close, and he turned to see that Peter had let himself in. Brows set low and straight, he wore a determined look. Nathan sat up, wiping his eyes, and opened his mouth, but there was nothing he could think to say. He didn't know if he could ever find the words to explain what he had seen and felt or why he was so affected now.

Fortunately, Peter didn't seem interested in words. He approached the bed, gently settled himself down beside Nathan, and pulled him into his arms. Nathan laid frozen at first, stunned and unsure. But the warmth from Peter quickly thawed his paralysis, and he buried his face into the fabric of Peter's shirt, pressing his forehead into the firmness of his chest. Peter, chin resting on Nathan's crown, hugged him tighter. A dam broke within Nathan, and he wept.

He wept for Mr. Millican and for the void he felt within himself. He wept knowing that he would be leaving Jude and Peter in a matter of weeks. And he wept because he knew now, beyond a doubt, that he loved Peter. Nothing had ever terrified him so much. Being this close to Peter now was like being inches from death. But the idea of being apart from him frightened him even more.

The scent of Peter and the heat radiating from him filled Nathan's senses, and the emptiness inside him lessened. The affair in Mr. Millican's room felt farther away. In fact, everything beyond his bed ceased to exist entirely. All that mattered was this very moment, being here with Peter.

Gradually, Nathan's sobs quieted, and his breath calmed. In the wake of his tears, peace washed over him like gentle waves upon a shore. In Peter's arms, he found a remarkable sense of rightness.

Peter rubbed slow, soothing circles onto his back with his thumb. "Get some sleep. I'll be right here," he said softly.

His voice sounded far away to Nathan as exhaustion had already begun to overtake him. But the distant reassurance that Peter would be there with him brought a faint smile to his face. He sighed contentedly and relented to the pull of sleep. Just before slipping into a deep and dreamless slumber, Nathan thought he felt the light press of lips atop his head, but his somnolent mind was unreliable. It must have been his imagination.

21

Nathan woke late the following morning feeling thoroughly rested. Jude brought him tea in bed and drew back his curtains. As the sunlight filled the room, the day before came back to him slowly. His heart sank upon realizing that Peter had been with him before and was now gone. He remembered his epiphany, just before falling asleep, regarding his feelings for Peter, and a concerning thought crossed his mind. Had he been speaking in his sleep? A cold knot of worry twisted in his gut.

"Good morning," Jude said. There was a hint of worry in her voice. "How are you feeling?"

"Better, thanks. I needed the rest. How are you?"

"Also much improved after a good night's sleep. After all the time we spent awake with Mr. Millican, the exhaustion caught up with me. I was in bed before six last night."

"I'm glad to hear that," Nathan smiled as best he could. "Was Dr. Beverley by?"

"Yes. And he pronounced him dead. The clocks have been stopped and the mirrors covered. He had no remaining family, so there was no one to contact besides your parents. I already sent them a telegram. They'll be here this evening."

Nathan sat up straight, nearly spilling his tea. "My God. Today?"

"That's right. The funeral will be tomorrow."

It only made sense that his parents would be on their way, but it hadn't occurred to him at any point yesterday that Mr. Millican's passing would mean their early arrival. He hadn't seen or heard from his father since the incident at their London home eight months ago. The idea that today he would be in the same room as him made his stomach lurch.

Jude seemed to see the quiet distress on his face. She sat on the bed and took one of his hands in hers. "It's going to be alright. I know you can do this. And if it feels like too much at times, remember that you're not alone. I'll be here, all right?"

Nathan relaxed slightly. "Thank you, Jude."

She smiled at him. Then, a thought anxiously lit up in her eyes and she turned away, chewing her lip. "I, um, was wanting to ask you. About yesterday…"

"Oh," he shrank, embarrassed. "I'm sorry. I must have given you a terrible fright."

"No, no. It isn't that, please don't apologize. I only wanted to know… You saw him pass on, didn't you? You saw the moment that Mr. Millican died?"

He stared at her apprehensively, before giving a sheepish nod. "Yes. I did."

"And—And he *went* somewhere. Is that right? Could you see it? What was it like?"

Her eyes were wide and hopeful. Nathan suddenly recalled her departed love John and realized that she wanted to know for his sake. He squeezed her hand and smiled. "It was the most brilliant light I've ever seen. And an ever-present sense of peace. There's truly nothing in this life that compares."

Jude smiled, chin trembling and eyes glistening. She released a long breath that ended in a wet laugh. "Sorry," she retrieved her handkerchief and blotted her tears. "I can't tell you how comforted I am, hearing that. Thank you."

Nathan moved the tea tray to the side and then pulled her into a hug. She seemed startled by this at first, but quickly recovered and hugged him tightly in return. He couldn't remember when they had last shared a hug. Peter's penchant for them seemed to be rubbing off on him.

As if hearing the mention of Peter in his thoughts, Jude said, "I came in here earlier, but you were still asleep.

I saw that Peter had kept you company." A smile played on her lips.

"That's right. He's been a wonderful friend." Nathan tried to keep his expression as casual as possible, but the color in his cheeks betrayed him.

She stood and grabbed the tea tray from the bed. "Yes, I should say so," she agreed. "But I can't help but wonder if perhaps there is something more. Something more…profound than friendship."

Nathan spluttered. His face was burning.

"Oh goodness, you're looking a bit feverish," she said wryly. "Are you feeling all right?"

"I'm fine," he said primly. "And I can assure you, there is nothing but the deepest fraternal affection between Peter and I."

"Of course," she said, looking all too pleased. "I hope you didn't take offense. I was only making an observation. It was rather sweet, seeing you two fast asleep. You both seemed very content together. Before I accidentally woke Peter, that is. He heard my footsteps as I was trying to leave. Seemed rather bashful about the whole thing. I told him he didn't need to be. Not with me."

She winked at him, then spun around and marched out of the room with the tray. Nathan watched her go and marveled. He doubted that her insinuations regarding Peter held water—he had been in love with a woman, after all—but her assumptions about him had been correct. He wondered to himself how long she'd known. It seemed to him that she may have known before even he himself did. He couldn't help but smile. In some ways, she saw so much more than anyone else.

The entire staff was neatly dressed and groomed, more so than usual, when Lord and Lady Hambleton arrived. Everyone stood outside of the house in uniform lines as their carriage approached the house. Nathan stood at the forefront, feeling sick with nerves and smiling with tight lips.

William, the footman, opened the carriage door and Nathan's mother stepped out first. She was in a black dress appropriate for mourning and wore her usual excessive amount of jewelry—bracelets, rings, dangling earrings, a broach, and a necklace. She also sported a large, extravagant hat with several long plumes.

"Nathaniel!" she cried with arms outstretched.

Some tension left his body. "Mother, it's so good to see you." She pulled him into a tight hug, her jewelry jangling loudly. She held him for a long time. One of her hat's feathers tickled his neck, but he hardly cared.

Then, just behind her, the imposing shape of Nathan's father stepped out of the carriage accompanied by a steady, low grating sound that set Nathan's teeth on edge. It was a noise like distant thunder with a shrill undercurrent like squeaking rusted metal. It hung around his father at all times in the same way that a cloud of familiar, comforting perfume hung around his mother. Only Nathan seemed to notice it.

He pulled away from his mother and looked at him. His father was a tall man with grave features. He always appeared to be scowling, and his icy grey eyes brought a chill to whomever they fell upon. How someone as warm as Nathan's mother could marry a man as cold as his father had always confounded him.

Lord Hambleton didn't spare Nathan so much as a passing glance. He approached Jude immediately. "Mrs. Fairchild, I see you've kept this place standing despite this year's…challenges." The word "challenges" dripped with disdain.

"Yes, my lord," she said neutrally.

He eyed the staff for a moment. "Someone is currently with Mr. Millican, I trust."

"Yes, my lord. Our new groundskeeper. Would your lordship like to see Mr. Millican now?"

"Tomorrow. We've had a long journey. I'll be retiring early after dinner."

"Of course, my lord. I've spoken with Mrs. Blake and dinner will be ready shortly."

Jude led Lord Hambleton into the house. Nathan's mother turned to him then, the worry on her face thinly disguised by a forced smile. "Well, you know how he is. He'll warm up in time."

"Yes. Yes, I do know how he is."

22

Dinner was painfully quiet. Nathan's mother made one or two attempts at conversation with no success.

"Nathaniel, how've you been managing here without a valet? Has the footman filled in?"

"No, I dress and shave myself actually. And Mrs. Fairchild trims my hair."

"Does she?" she said enthusiastically. "Well, she does an excellent job. Wouldn't you say so, Victor?"

Nathan's father didn't look up from his plate. Dinner continued in silence, broken only by William, who brought in the next courses. When their meal was finished, Lord Hambleton stood, told his wife he was retiring for the night, and left without another word.

"Would you care to join me for a brandy in the parlor, Nathaniel?" his mother asked brightly, as if all were right with the world.

"Now, what was all that commotion about with Dr. Mathis?" She took a sip of her brandy and leaned back into the couch.

"Your guess is as good as mine," Nathan said smoothly. "I merely told him that we were short-staffed and not in a position to properly host. Mr. Millican had only recently taken his fall." His mother made a doleful face at the mention of the late estate manager. "So, I arranged to have him stay at the village inn."

"Well, that was rather kind of you."

"I thought so, too, but he was irate," he shrugged, seemingly at a loss and took a sip of his brandy.

She appeared to ponder this, absently twisting a large, gem-studded ring around her finger with her thumb and watching him with keen eyes as if trying to decide whose story she believed more—his or Dr. Mathis's. "The doctor also said you made some rather abhorrent accusations against him."

He sighed. "You see, it was a misunderstanding. I told him, in jest, that it was fortunate his recent treatment cured me because my years of persistent illness were surely tarnishing his reputation."

"Cured?" she asked. "How do you mean?"

"I mean, the doctor had prescribed me a six-week long treatment over spring, and it worked like nothing else. It made a remarkable difference. He did seem surprised, though, that his prescription worked so effectively. But I daresay, the change is obvious to anyone who knew me prior."

"Yes," she said, squinting slightly. "There is something different about you."

Nathan smiled, "You see? I believe the change was a bit jarring for the doctor, that's all. Though, he did react so strongly… I have to wonder if maybe he is under some sort of stress in his life. Perhaps, the demands of his practice are becoming too much for him in his older age."

His mother conceded the theory with a hum. "Perhaps you're right. He did seem terribly stressed when I saw him last."

A comfortable moment of silence fell over them as they sipped their drinks, and Nathan took the opportunity to pivot the conversation. "Why hasn't Daniel come?"

"He wanted to, of course, but he is so busy with wedding preparations that he couldn't afford the time away. There's not only the nuptials to consider but also the honeymoon, and," she sighed and waved a hand vaguely, "whatever else."

"I've been wanting to ask. What is it exactly that you don't like about his fiancée?"

"Oh, she's perfectly pleasant," she said bitterly. "But it isn't an advantageous wedding for our family. There's no fortune to speak of. No promise of future inheritance. Nothing."

"Mother!" He was surprised at her. In many ways she was a romantic, but then there were times like this where a calculating, unsentimental part of her personality revealed itself. Perhaps, he thought, this was the thing that endeared her to his father. "So, you mean to say that it's a marriage of *love* rather than advantage. Can that really be such a bad thing?"

She scoffed, "You sound like Daniel."

"Mother, come now. Finance and investing are Daniel's forte. I think if anyone would see the necessity for a marriage of convenience it would be him. Clearly, he believes our family will manage perfectly well without one." She scowled at him but said nothing which meant she was struggling to refute his reasoning. "And as such, I would think you'd be happy for your son to have a chance at love and happiness. I'm certainly happy for him."

She glowered at him with indignant, pursed lips, but he knew it was only an act. Her hard expression was beginning to crack at the edges.

"Nathaniel, how is it that you *always* make me sound like such a monster!" she said theatrically, unable to hide her smile.

"Not *always*!"

"Yes, you do!" she insisted. "Oh, but I'm sure you're right. Daniel certainly isn't yielding to my wishes, so I suppose that all a mother in my position can hope is that her son's fiancée makes him happy and gives him a healthy family. Which, I'm sure she will. She's a charming, strong girl who will make an excellent wife someday, I have no doubt."

Nathan grinned. "Something tells me that's the nicest thing you've ever said about her."

"Don't look so pleased," she huffed. "To be frank, she never bothered me nearly as much as she did your—" She stopped herself abruptly, clamping her lips together tightly.

"As she did Father," he finished.

His mother looked down at her glass, twisting the stem slowly between her fingers. "You know, I really did agree with him at first," she explained quickly as if defending herself. "Some sort of advantage to come from Daniel's wedding—social, pecuniary, or otherwise—would have been ideal, after all, for the family. But, overtime, I could see that Daniel was truly happy with her. What kind of mother would I be if I couldn't see that? Of course, then again, what kind of wife would I be if I didn't stand beside my husband?"

"So, you've been attempting to undermine their engagement to appease Father."

"Yes and no," she closed her eyes and sighed. "My real aim has been to keep peace within the family. Or, at least, that's what I've been letting myself believe. You see, Daniel is well aware of his father's opinions. And as such, he knows that if he proceeds with this wedding anyway, it stands to cause a rift between them. Perhaps Daniel is willing to take that risk, but I do not want to lose another son. It's been unbearable not seeing you, Nathaniel. And I hope that when you return to London with us next month, things will be better than last time. But, if not…" She shook the thought from her head and took a steadying breath. "You may choose to judge me for my meddling in Daniel's love life if you wish, but I've only been doing what I can to keep my sons in my life. Nothing more."

Nathan wanted to retort, to tell her frankly that his father was the reason their family threatened to fall apart, not Daniel's choice of fiancée or his own peculiar gifts. But he saw the hurt on her face, despite her best effort to conceal it. Between her husband and her sons, she stood in a precarious position.

"I don't judge you."

She turned to him with surprise in her eyes. "You don't?"

"No, Mother, I don't. Though, I am surprised that you had to intervene at all. If Father truly dislikes Daniel's fiancée so much, why hasn't he put his foot down more firmly? Threatened to cut him off financially?"

She laughed, "He wouldn't dare! Daniel is more business savvy than he is. He absolutely depends on him to manage the family's accounts."

Nathan grinned. "Well played, Daniel. He always was a rather sharp chess player, you know."

"Yes, well, your father is a terribly sore loser."

"He's only a loser in this situation if he chooses to be."

She smiled at him fondly then and put a gentle hand on his face. "I really have missed you, my dear."

"I know," he smiled in kind, "I've missed you, also."

"It's under dreadful circumstances that we've come early, but I'm glad to be here with you. Though, speaking of," she rose to her feet, "it was quite a long journey, and there is a challenging day ahead of us tomorrow. I should be off to bed."

He stood with her and took her empty brandy glass to the gallery tray on the nearby table.

Just before leaving, she turned to him and said, "Oh, and I would appreciate you not mentioning any of this to your father."

"I wouldn't dream of it."

She looked at him tenderly. "It's good to see you looking so well, Nathaniel. Goodnight, dear."

"Goodnight, Mother."

———

In his room, Nathan readied himself for bed as calmly as he could. The noise from before—the low but somehow piercing rumbled that followed his father—carried through the house. He'd heard it all evening and had been doing his best to swallow down the building pressure inside him.

It was a sound he knew too well. Ever-present since he was a small boy, but considerably worse in the years since returning from university. It wore him down over his lifetime and finally broke him last autumn. Hearing it again now and thinking back on that night months ago made him irritable and tense. He didn't know how he would manage back in London, surrounded by the unrelenting presence of his father at all times.

He laid in bed, lamp still lit, wondering if Peter would be by tonight or if Jude had warned him against it while Lord Hambleton was in the house. He hated how different the house felt since his parents arrived. The whole staff seemed uneasy. Jude was rigid and formal and often out-of-sight when she wasn't immediately needed. Peter hadn't yet met Lord Hambleton, and being the groundskeeper, he might not at all, but Nathan worried that if they were to cross paths his father's shrewd eyes would find fault with him right away.

Then came a small knock at the door. Nathan sat up eagerly. The door opened, and Peter peered in. Nathan smiled, and he motioned for him to come in.

"I know I shouldn't be here," Peter whispered, sitting on the edge of the bed. "Mrs. Fairchild said I better not, but I wanted to see you."

"I'm glad you did. I wanted to see you, too."

Peter fidgeted with his fingers. "I-I'm sorry I didn't say anything this morning. You see, I overslept and was in a hurry. I wanted to say goodbye and to make sure you were all right, but I also didn't want to wake you."

"It's all right," Nathan assured him. "In fact, I wanted to thank you. For yesterday. You're—" *Grounding. Intoxicating. Perfect.* "You're a wonderful friend."

Peter smiled and dropped his eyes. "I feel the same way. I can't say I've ever had a friend like you before."

Nathan's heart flipped excitedly in his chest, and he sternly reminded himself not to let his own feelings cloud his judgment. Hope was a dangerous thing. While he had accepted the existence of his feelings for Peter, he didn't dare act on them. They would only ever be friends, and that was enough. He would rather have Peter in his life as a friend than nothing at all.

"Me neither," he said, voice trailing off as he stared at Peter's hands and arms and imagined them wrapped around him again. There was a pull within his body, aching to close the gap between them.

Peter looked up and held Nathan's gaze, steady and unbroken. Silence reigned between them for a moment as they seemed on the edge of an unspoken conversation. Nathan's heart fluttered expectantly again.

Then Peter blinked as if coming out of a daze and said suddenly, "How are you feeling today? Any better?"

Nathan blinked, too. "Oh… Yes! Much better. Or, as good as I can be in the company of my parents anyway."

"I know they've arrived, but I haven't met them yet. The whole house feels a bit more tense now, I must admit."

"Yes, my father has that effect on his surroundings."

"Will you be playing at the funeral tomorrow? Your violin, I mean? I've heard you're a very skilled player."

"Oh," Nathan said sheepishly. "No, I won't be. I don't play for others anymore."

"Why not?"

He sighed. "When I was fourteen, I played for a few friends of the family once at our London home. A rather ambitious piece by Paganini, but I'd been practicing tirelessly and was excited to perform. When I played, at first, everything was normal. I felt confident, in fact. It was the best rendition of that piece I'd ever played. But then, the way my mother tells it, the piece *changed.*

"I had stopped playing Paganini without realizing it and begun playing something else entirely. And whatever it was had a deep effect on our guests. The woman—I forget her name now; we never saw her again after that night—she began to cry. I stopped playing at once, of course, but it was too late. She was inconsolable, saying that the piece reminded her of her daughter, who died of pneumonia four years prior. Her husband was angry and accused me of purposefully upsetting them. They both left the party, and my father was furious with me. He told me I could never play again. My mother eventually convinced him to let me practice in private, but I've never played for an audience since."

"My God…" Peter said with awe. "You're full of surprises, aren't you?"

"I suppose that's one way of saying it."

He looked at Nathan then with mischief in his eyes. "Would you play for me sometime?"

"Peter! Heavens, no!"

"Oh, *please*?"

"I can't believe you'd ask after everything I've just told you," he said incredulously.

"I understand the risks," Peter raised his hands in a pacifying gesture. "And if you really don't want to, then I won't press you. But I sincerely want to hear you play. You've dedicated so much time to the craft, it's really a shame you can't share it with anyone."

Nathan stared at him disapprovingly, but Peter's honest and eager face chipped away at his resolve. He sighed, "I'll *consider* it."

Peter grinned from ear to ear. "Really? You mean that?"

"As of right now, I'm *just* considering it, but yes, I mean it," he was smiling now, too. Some part of him wondered if Peter realized that he was his greatest weakness.

"Take all the time you need. I don't mind waiting."

It occurred to Nathan then, that since he'd been with Peter, the terrible sound of his father's presence had quieted. The tension in his jaw and shoulders had slackened, and for the first time in hours, he felt at peace. He thought to himself then that he'd never survive in London without Peter.

23

Mr. Millican's funeral service was held late morning at the small cemetery near the village church. The sun was shining, and the birds chirped brightly, which Nathan found deeply inappropriate. The vicar held a brief but poignant service, and then Mr. Millican's coffin was lowered into its grave. Nathan tossed in the first flower and others followed suit.

After the funeral, he stepped into the carriage behind his mother and father, wishing to himself that he could make the trip back home on foot with the staff and walk alongside Jude and Peter. But he didn't dare risk anything so unconventional with his father present.

The household was still in mourning, so staff did minimal work for the remainder of the day. Nathan was able to excuse himself from his parents' company and stayed in his chambers, leaving only for dinner. His father had been at the house for less than a day and already Nathan couldn't wait to be away from him. Bitter panic rose in the back of his throat when he thought about his impending return to London.

The following day, the staff was expected to return to their normal duties, albeit wearing black armbands. The air of grief was already beginning to dissipate. Nathan felt that it was too soon to behave as if everything were normal again, but he didn't have a say in the matter.

For the rest of the week, he endured uncomfortable, tense meals and the grating noise of his father's presence. He barely saw Jude as she was busy catering to Lord and Lady Hambleton. In fact, she no longer woke him in the mornings. Nathan's father had promptly instructed William, the footman, to perform the duties of valet as he apparently felt it was inappropriate that his son did not have one.

The only peace he found was in the evening when Peter stopped by to speak with him. One night, Nathan told him that he wanted to show his mother the greenhouse. He was excited to show her the beautiful work Peter had put into it, and besides that, it was a good excuse to be out of the house and away from his father.

"It's best that you aren't there when I show her. Though, I wish you could be," Nathan said. "My parents believe staff should remain as invisible as possible."

"It's all right," Peter assured him, smiling with a twinge of sadness. "I knew things would be different once they arrived."

———

"That one is called *Alocasia calidora.* It's native to southeast Asia. And that one is *Codiaeum variegatum.* Such brilliant colors, don't you think?" Nathan strolled with his mother through the greenhouse, pointing out the different plants he learned to care for under Peter's guidance. Fuchsia, Kentia palms, Maidenhair ferns, Jerusalem cherries, Philodendrons.

His mother put a hand on his arm, "Nathaniel, my dear, I do appreciate your enthusiasm, but my mind is positively bursting with plant names right now, and I'm not sure it can hold more. Perhaps, we could sit for a moment. I need to catch my breath."

He blushed, "Yes, of course. Sorry, Mother. I'd gotten carried away."

She took a seat on a bench nearby. "No, no, it's quite all right, darling. In fact, I'm quite impressed. When did you take such an interest in botany?"

"Just recently. The new groundskeeper has been teaching me about the different species and how to care for them."

"The new groundskeeper," she tilted her head in thought. "Yes, I remember now. Mr. Audrey mentioned him months ago. Young fellow, if I remember correctly."

"That's right," Nathan smiled. "Peter."

"Yes, Peter! That's it," his mother said cheerfully. "Well, he's certainly done remarkable work. The greenhouse hasn't looked this handsome in many years." A shadow passed over her face. It was true; for the past few years, the greenhouse hadn't been as attractive as usual, and it was due to Mr. Millican's age.

He cleared his throat. "Do you remember how Daniel and I would dig through the flowerbeds as boys looking for that old biscuit tin?"

"Oh, I certainly do," a smile returned to her face. "I would get so angry about the mess you two would make. But Mr. Millican never seemed to mind all that much. He was always so patient with you both."

"He was," he agreed thoughtfully. "Believe it or not, Peter and I found that very biscuit tin when he was clearly out the greenhouse."

"You're joking!"

"No, it had been buried here for over a decade. Unearthing it was like stepping back in time. It was incredible. I think it would make a wonderful gift for Daniel. Perhaps a wedding gift."

"I think that's a splendid idea. What a marvelous thing to rediscover after all this time. Between the treasure and recent botanical interests, you seem to really have found your place in the greenhouse."

Nathan laughed. "Yes, I suppose you're right."

"And I take it you and Peter have become close since he's arrived?"

"Yes, I'd say so," he said as neutrally as possible, trying hard to suppress memories of sleeping in Peter's arms for fear of flushing. "He's become a good friend."

"A *friend*?" she said a bit too enthusiastically. "Nathaniel, that's wonderful to hear. You know, you always did have trouble making friends as a boy."

"Yes, Mother, I know…" he grumbled, resisting the urge to roll his eyes.

"And he's taught you so much, too," she gestured to the plants around them. "Though, it is quite a shame you'll be returning to the city. I'd have him relocated to our home in London if we had need for a groundskeeper, but as it is, I'm afraid the poor man would be bored senseless with nothing to do. Besides, I'm sure Daniel would appreciate his services here. He's done simply wonderful work."

In the span of a sentence, Nathan's heart had swelled with sudden hope that Peter could join him in London only for his dream to be promptly followed by crushing disappointment. Oblivious, his mother had already moved on from the subject.

"Speaking of, I'd love to see the rest of the grounds. The wedding reception will be outside, you know. I'd like to make sure that everything is more or less ready."

Nathan rose to his feet and led his mother out of the greenhouse while she prattled away about the nuptials, but her voice was distant to him. He thought only of Peter and their inevitable goodbye.

24

"Victor, darling, it was really most impressive. Our Nathaniel spoke like a proper botanist. Rattling off the scientific names of things and how to care for them. It was remarkable."

It was lunch the following day, and Nathan's mother was making a concerted effort to engage him and his father in conversation. His father had not said a single word to him or even looked at him since arriving. In some ways, Nathan appreciated not having to speak with him. Their conversations were never productive. However, after nearly a week of being ignored, his blood was beginning to boil. For all his father's talk of manners and common decency, he clearly didn't adhere to his own philosophies. It was all too easy for him to bend the rules for himself, Nathan thought, all the while holding those around him to an absurdly high standard.

"And the violets are lovely at the moment. They're in full bloom, but Nathaniel said they won't last much longer before the summer heat withers them. Perhaps, you could accompany him on a tour of the greenhouse sometime. Maybe soon?"

Nathan shot his mother a dismayed look across the table. He was prepared to contend with awkward conversation over lunch with her supervision, but he was not interested in an outing with his father. Especially not in the greenhouse. That had become something of sacred space to him. It was a place that reminded him of time spent with Peter, and he did not want his father spoiling it.

Fortunately, his father didn't seem keen on the idea either. "Perhaps, not," he told her coolly.

She pressed the matter further, "But, I think you might appreciate seeing the fruits of Nathaniel's labor. He really possesses an aptitude."

Without any warning, he slammed his utensils down onto his plate, and both Nathan and his mother started.

"How wonderful," he said with bitter sarcasm. "My son, the amateur farmer. I send him here to focus on his health so he may one day rejoin society as a civilized man, and he spends his time taking up a most *worthwhile* trade. Truly, a man possessing the Hambleton name and reputation is well-suited to a life as a goddamn farmhand."

"*Victor!*" his mother shouted, appalled.

Nathan stood from the table abruptly, his chair falling backwards onto the carpet, and made for the door.

"Nathaniel!" a stern, booming voice called out behind him. "Sit back down at once."

He stopped. It was the first time his father had spoken to him since he sent him away from London. He whirled around.

"*Now* you acknowledge me," Nathan spat. "Eight months without so much as a letter or telegram to wish me well on Christmas or my birthday. And then, after all that time, you arrive here and greet the housekeeper but not your son. For nearly a week, you act as though I don't exist."

His father rose to his feet too, his nostrils flared and jaw set tight. "Don't you *dare* speak to me that way."

"Why?" he asked derisively. "Because you'll think poorly of me? Tell me, Father, how ever will I endure your disapproval?" The last thing he saw before turning away was his father's face, red and irate. His eyes were wide with fury, and the image reminded Nathan of that night in October. It sent a shiver down his spine, but he carried on, marching out of the dining room and slamming the door shut behind him.

"*NATHANIEL!*"

He heard his father's yell carry through the house. Jude emerged from the hallway, all but running, with an alarmed look on her face and nearly collided with him. When she saw him, she stopped, and glanced wildly between him and the direction of the dining room.

"What—?" she asked helplessly. The distant sound of a dish breaking rang out, and she put a hand over her mouth.

Nathan walked past her without comment and continued to the front entrance. He was too frightened to slow down, as well as too angry. If he returned to his father now, he knew he would not be able to stop himself from saying more spiteful things, and the potential consequences were unspeakable.

He burst through the doors and out into the warm afternoon, but he didn't stop. Following the pathway behind the house, Nathan marched past the barn and took the small footpath to the treeline just as he had on the day of the picnic. He was nearly to the gap in the hedgerow when he heard footsteps in the grass behind him, approaching quickly. Fearing they were his father's, he whirled around defensively, scowling and clenching his hands at his sides ready for a confrontation. But it was not his father. It was Peter. His eyes were wide and confused, his brows drawn together in worry.

Peter opened his mouth but seemed surprised at the sight of anger in Nathan's face and fumbled over his words. He gestured back behind himself, "I-I saw you from the gardens. What's wrong?"

Nathan's hostility immediately dissipated. "Peter! I'm sorry, I thought you— It's just that my father and I—"

"Your father? What did he do?" He stood up straighter and set his jaw, seemingly prepared to fight Lord Hambleton on his behalf. The idea was both flattering and alarming. His father was a powerful man in many respects, and it would be best for Peter if they didn't cross swords.

"We had an argument is all," he explained hastily. "And I couldn't stand to be in the house with him any longer. I came out here to cool my head."

Peter seemed to relax some. "I see." He nodded toward the gap in the trees then, "Where were you headed?"

"Honestly, I don't know. Maybe to the picnic spot again, if my anger carried me that far."

"If I may, I have a better suggestion," he said with a glimmer in his eyes. "Wait here. I'll only be gone a moment." He turned and jogged back to the barn.

Despite his simmering frustrations, Nathan smiled as he watched him go. Life with Peter felt different. Things felt easier, somehow. Like living with the unshakable conviction that everything would turn out all right in the end.

25

Peter returned a moment later with a saddle blanket under his arm and led Nathan beyond the estate's perimeter. They walked along the outside of the treeline, down toward the mouth of the lake, and then followed the small stream that fed into it away from the estate. They carried on in comfortable silence. Nathan wasn't sure what Peter had in mind, but he didn't feel the need to ask. He trusted him.

As they walked beside the stream, it gradually widened and deepened. The sound of moving water soothed the remaining tension in Nathan's body. He looked up at the modest canopy of trees that sprouted along the banks and watched the sunshine shimmer through the leaves. The shade was a blessing as temperatures had risen considerably since their picnic nearly two months ago. Nathan wondered how many more days the violets in the greenhouse would last.

"This is the spot," Peter said at last. They'd reached a wide and gentle area in the stream's current. There was adequate tree coverage and a large, flat stone at the water's edge, on which Peter unfurled the saddle blanket. Then, he began unlacing his boots and glanced back at Nathan with a smile, "Care for a swim?"

Nathan, immediately aware of the implications, was struck with an overwhelming mix of anticipation and fear. "Swim? Are you being serious?"

"Absolutely," he said, tucking his socks neatly into his boots. "What better way is there to cool one's head?"

"But I haven't brought along a bathing costume." Nathan tugged anxiously at his fingers.

Peter gave him a funny smile, "There isn't anyone around. And frankly, I can't imagine swimming with clothes on."

"You mean you've never worn a bathing costume before?" He already knew the answer to this but was stalling for time, trying desperately to think of ways to escape.

"Never," Peter said, standing now and stepping out of his trousers. "They're not something most farming families can afford. But we make do."

"I see," Nathan said absently, watching Peter peel off his shirt and start on the buttons of his underwear. He couldn't think of any reasonable excuses to remove himself from the situation. For a moment, he considered turning and leaving without a word, but he couldn't bring himself to do that to Peter. So, he slowly began taking off his own jacket and tried not to let his eyes wander.

The sound of fabric falling to the ground caught his attention and, against his better judgment, he glanced over to Peter, who was now fully undressed. His breath caught in his throat and butterflies fluttered in his head. He was dumbstruck, unable to think or move. He could do nothing but stare at the broad expanse of Peter's shoulders, the strong muscles of his back, and the elegant curve of his spine leading down to firm hindquarters and solid thighs. The skin of his torso and legs, untouched by the sun, appeared fair and soft, and he wondered how it might feel to run his fingertips along his shoulder blades.

Peter turned back to him then, quickly snapping him out of his daze. He looked away immediately but was certain Peter had seen his eyes on him. He kept his face down as he began unlacing his own shoes, hoping that his red-hot flush wasn't noticeable.

"Are you coming?" Peter asked.

"Um, yes," Nathan said without looking at him. "In a moment. Go on ahead."

He heard the slosh of water followed by a sharp inhale and glanced up. Peter was slowly wading out into the stream, facing away from him.

"It is a bit cold, I won't lie," he called out of his shoulder. "But not terrible. Rather refreshing, I'd say."

A shiver visibly rippled through Peter's muscles, and in a few short strides, he was in the middle of the stream, the water not quite high enough to reach the dimples of his lower back. Nathan had removed his trousers and was making progress on his shirt, watching Peter all the while. Though unable to stop himself looking, he felt a deep guilt in his heart for indulging his desires. It was shameful to be watching a friend with lustful eyes. If Peter only knew, he would've never undressed in his company.

Without warning, Peter submerged himself fully in the stream and swiftly sprang back up, gasping for air and laughing. "Yes, that is definitely refreshing." He turned to look at Nathan, grinning widely, water dripping from every inch of him.

Nathan smiled back with as much sincerity he could muster, trying hard not to follow the droplets rolling down Peter's chest and stomach, catching in the thin trail of hair leading from his navel downwards to thick, dark curls that disappeared under the water's surface. He was in only his undergarments now and began to shake as he unfastened his buttons. Finally, once they were all opened, he slid his arms out and let the last of his clothes fall to the ground. Some distant part of his mind noted—rather obviously—that he was standing naked outside, something he most certainly had never done before. But whatever sense of liberation might've come with the experience was thoroughly overshadowed by the mortification he felt over his body.

Don't turn around. Don't let him see.

Peter was crouched in the water and leaning back, looking up at the tree canopy, while Nathan stood at the stream's edge unable to make himself step in. He stared down at the crystal-clear water, but his thoughts were far away, back to that haunting October night at his family's London home, reliving the memory, the terror. His mother's screaming, his father's hate-filled eyes, the sound of glass crushing under weight. He could hear the maddening sound again. The terrible, shrill shrieking, unceasing and inescapable. His fingers began to tremble.

Then, Peter's voice brought him back to the present again. "Nathan?" He was standing now in the stream and watching him with concern. "Are you all right?"

At the sound of his name, Nathan started. "Please, don't look at me," he said hastily, turning away and reaching for his clothes.

"What? What are you—?" Peter fell silent behind him, and Nathan knew he had seen. It was too late. He helplessly dropped his clothes to the ground and began to cry. The shame and embarrassment were too great.

Water swashed behind him followed by the soft steps of bare feet on earth. Nathan could feel Peter's eyes on him, and it made him cry harder. Without a word, Peter reached out and gently took his hand and guided him over to the saddle blanket. They sat down together, side by side, and Peter said nothing, only waited. Nathan's quiet sobs carried on the warm summer breeze like whispers and mingled with the crisp, bright melody of moving water. Eventually, the stream's easy current became the only sound in the air around them, save for the occasional sniff.

"What happened?" Peter asked in a low voice. "How did you get those scars?"

Since they had healed, Nathan spent very little time observing the scars in the mirror. Only once or twice. The last time had been in December, but he could recall them vividly in his mind. Thin, pink lines scattered across his shoulders and back. They were mostly small, but there were dozens of them. Some curved, some twisted at sharp angles. Others were only small dots and dashes—roseate punctuation upon a flesh-colored page.

"It was that night," Nathan said, wiping his eyes. "That one in October. The reason for my father sending me away. It was..." He dropped his head and sighed. "It's ridiculous. The whole damned thing. *I'm* ridiculous."

"No, you're not. I wish you wouldn't say things like that." Peter stared at him sternly.

Nathan couldn't hold his gaze, so he looked down at his knees instead and took a breath. "When I was away at university, electricity had been added to our London home. We were the first in our neighborhood. My father... He champions invention and innovation. But there's this..." He paused, trying to place the word. "*Timbre* to electricity. It's difficult to describe. It's like feeling a charge in the air before lightning strikes. It's as much a physical sensation as it is a sound. As far as I'm aware, no one else seems to notice it, but for me, it's constant. In the house, it was always in the background.

"There is, however, another sound in the house at all times that only I seem to hear. It surrounds my father. It's a low rumbling, like thunder, but it's also somehow sharp and grating. For as long as I can remember that noise has followed him. It fills every inch of the home."

"My God... How did you sleep?"

"Poorly," he admitted. "It wasn't as apparent when I was young. It's grown more noticeable, more...insistent over the years. It's been especially unbearable since I've returned from university. It's the electricity, I think. It seems to amplify the sound, and the low, grating rumble I'd grown accustomed to had become a train whistle, howling at all hours of the day." He sighed again and ran his fingers through his hair. "This all sounds mad."

"Please," Peter reached out and rested a hand on his thigh, "Just tell me. I want to know."

The touch sent a shiver through Nathan's chest to his loins. He willed himself to ignore the feeling of Peter's hand for fear that his own body would betray him. "Well, unsurprisingly, I took every opportunity to leave the house. I'd frequent museums, parks, libraries, shops. But I always had to go back home at some point, and the sound awaited me. My sleep suffered, and eventually, I developed terrible, persistent migraines, the worst I've ever experienced, and I could no longer leave the house.

That's when things became truly grim. There was no peace. Even if my father left the house for any reason, the noise still remained as an echo. I truly believed that I was going insane, and in retrospect, I was.

"One night—*the* night—my parents were hosting friends, while I lay in my bed, desperately trying to rest. I hadn't slept properly in months, and once the migraines started, I hadn't slept at all in three days. I've never felt that way before. I was so *angry* and couldn't stop myself from crying. It went on for hours. The visions I have, they became terrifying and sinister, and I felt that I was being watched at all times by something. It was a waking nightmare. Apparently, in my hysteria, I ripped apart one of my pillows with a letter opener, but I don't recall doing it. Finally, I'd had enough. I grabbed a heavy book from my shelf, left my room, and began breaking all the lightbulbs in the hall, screaming and shouting like a madman. There was glass all over the carpet. And then… Then, I remember seeing my father, running towards me, fire burning in his eyes. He was beyond furious. He knocked the book from my hands and wrestled me to the ground, onto the glass, and I was kicking and yelling, and then he put his weight on me. At the time, I was only vaguely aware of the shards beneath me. A-And then, he tried— He…" His voice trembled. "He put his hands on my throat and pressed down hard, telling me through gritted teeth to be quiet. And I remember trying to breathe and trying to scream for help, but every utterance I made compelled him to tighten his grip. The last thing I remember was hearing my mother scream and the look in my father's eyes. It was pure hatred. Unbridled rage. He wanted me dead."

From the corner of his eye, Nathan saw Peter, who had been watching him as he spoke, turn away. He glanced at him. Peter's jaw was clenched tightly, his nostrils flared with each breath. He stared out at the stream, a darkness in his eyes.

"If he ever touches you again…" he shook his head slightly and let the thought hang in the air between them, unfinished. "I don't think I can bear to even look at him."

"Please don't do anything that might get you dismissed. I need you here with me." Peter turned to look at him then, a question in his eyes, and Nathan worried that he'd revealed too much of himself. He dropped his gaze back to his knees and tried to push the conversation forward, "Besides, what's done is done. And in some ways, I blame myself as much as I do him."

"Don't," Peter said forcefully, surprising Nathan. "It wasn't your fault."

Under the weight of Peter's gaze, he felt himself start to blush. "Maybe you're right. I suppose in either case it doesn't serve me to spend a lifetime wondering if there was anything I could've done differently. Maybe it's enough to live with the memory. And the scars."

"Do they still hurt?"

"No. Only my pride. But there are worse things in this life than ugliness."

"There's nothing ugly about you."

At Peter's words, Nathan became suddenly conscious of their propinquity. He could feel the heat emanating from Peter and the soft brush of his breath on his shoulder every time he exhaled. The awareness of his strong body was threatening Nathan with arousal. His mouth had gone dry, and his heart was racing. His own anatomy was dangerously close to revealing the truth of his feelings.

With a slow, tender hand, Peter reached out toward his scars. Knowing the touch would be too much for his eager, responsive body, Nathan grabbed his wrist.

"Please, don't," he pleaded. "I-I value our friendship so much. I don't want to ruin it." His heart was beating in his throat. If there was any doubt in Peter's mind before, he thought, there certainly wasn't now. He'd confessed. And Peter now knew that every friendly gesture and touch he'd shared with Nathan had served as temptation for him.

Surprise crossed Peter's face followed by deep hurt. Nathan felt himself crumble inside. It had been a gamble to confess, but he thought—hoped—Peter would understand. He hoped Peter could overlook this part of him just as he had overlooked so many of his shortcomings and oddities. But it was clear from the wounded expression on face that this was different.

Peter scrambled to his feet silently and grabbed his clothes. Nathan dropped his head and closed his eyes. He wanted desperately to say something, anything, that would assure Peter that they could return to being friends as they were before and that his feelings were nothing more than a temporary, unremarkable condition that would fade with time like a sunburn. But he could think of nothing to say. He only kept his eyelids shut, giving Peter the privacy and respect he deserved.

He heard hurried steps moving away from him and soon all he could hear was the prattling of the stream.

26

Nathan stayed seated on the saddle blanket long after Peter had left. He couldn't shake the look of hurt he saw in his eyes. Knowing that he was the cause of that hurt made Nathan hate himself. He hated his damned body and the longing he felt for Peter. He thought endlessly about ways he could make it right, but he came up short. If Peter didn't want to be his friend, he would simply have to accept his decision as gracefully as possible.

Over the past months, Peter had become his reason for waking up in the mornings, for finding beauty in the world around him. Peter had reacquainted him with hope and tenderness and levity. He helped him to see himself with kindness and understanding, something he had not ever been able to do alone. The thought that they may not speak together again made his stomach feel sick.

He trusted that Peter wouldn't disclose his romantic proclivities to others, but this thought did little to comfort him. Imagining life without Peter made his skin itch and his heart feel unsettled in his chest. If Nathan was a kite sailing high above the clouds, then Peter was the strong and steady stone to which he was tethered. Without him, he was destined to lose himself to the gales of life.

After some time sitting beside the stream, Nathan's posterior had grown numb, and he accepted that he would have to return to the house and face his father's fury. He stood and dressed slowly, allowing the circulation to return to his legs. As he pulled on his trousers, his mind returned to the memory of Peter's bare body. He berated himself for having such thoughts and wished more than anything that they would leave him altogether. He would pay any price to have them removed so that he could be like other men—like men better than himself.

Without haste, he made the trek back to the summer home. It was late afternoon now, the day still very much vibrant and alive, but its beauty was lost on him. He could think only of the misery he felt.

As he passed through the gap in the hedgerow, he was disturbed from his thoughts by an anxious figure walking quickly toward him. It was Jude, her face both worried and relieved.

"There you are!" She huffed, "I was prepared to scour the entire countryside looking for you. What on earth did you say to your father earlier? I've never seen him so angry!" Nathan opened his mouth, but she waved a hand. "Never mind, there isn't time now. You need to come with me. And look sharp!"

"What do you mean?"

"Don't you remember? Today's Thursday!"

Realization dawned on Nathan then and he blanched. He didn't need another reason for his father to be angry with him. "God help me, I'd completely forgotten! Are they already here?"

"No, but they will be soon. Everyone is waiting out front. Your mother sent me to find you and I searched everywhere I could think. Then, Peter told me that you both had gone for an impromptu swim, and you wanted to stay behind. You chose a mighty fine day for that!" she quipped. "Speaking of, Peter seemed upset. Did you two have an argument?" She shook her head and waved a hand again. "There isn't time for this, we have to go *now!*"

They hurried to the servants' entrance and passed through the house as quickly as they could, all but running, until finally arriving at the entrance hall. Jude stopped Nathan for a moment, placing her hands firmly on his shoulders, and looked him over.

"Tuck in your shirt," she said as she adjusted his collar and straightened his jacket. "All right, you look fine now." She pulled open the door, and he walked calmly out, trying to keep his breath even after their run across the grounds.

The staff was already outside, standing in perfect rows. Nathan caught sight of Peter, but his eyes were downcast. At the sound of the door opening, Nathan's mother turned and looked immensely relieved to see him.

She held out a hand, "Come, darling, they're nearly here. Let's make a good impression, shall we? I'm sure they'll both appreciate a warm welcome."

In the distance, on the long road leading to the summer home, a carriage approached. Nathan took his place beside his mother. His father said nothing, but anger came off him in waves. The rumbling noise around him had taken on a quality that sounded like splintering wood. Nathan wanted to turn around and look at Peter, but he didn't risk it with his father standing nearby. Any step out of line was liable to cause his anger to boil over.

When the carriage finally arrived, William moved forward to open the door. Daniel stepped out first, looking tall and dapper as per usual. He shared a strong resemblance with Nathan, though not as thin and closer to their father's height. Upon seeing his brother, Daniel's face broke out into a broad smile.

"Nathan!" He said excitedly, arms outstretched. "How wonderful to see you!" He closed the space between them in a few long strides and pulled his brother into a tight embrace.

Nathan hugged him back, albeit a little surprised at the enthusiastic display of affection. That is not to say that they did not get along well as brothers, only that they were not typically sentimental. They'd always maintained a pleasantness and courtesy together, but in the same manner that one may have for a friend of a friend.

Daniel pulled away then and spoke in a quieter voice, "I didn't get the chance to see you off last year. I sincerely hope you've been well. I would've written, except…"

Their father cleared his throat loudly. "Daniel," he said tersely and gestured back to the carriage. "Where are your manners?"

Nathan looked between Daniel and his father. Had Daniel been forbidden from corresponding with him? Knowing his father, it seemed entirely probable. It was curious then that his mother hadn't also been prohibited. Unless, all this time, she really had been. Nathan glanced at her. She gave him a warning look with her eyes. *Do not speak of it to your father,* it said.

"Quite right, Father," Daniel replied with the faintest hint of a grimace on his face. He walked back to the carriage and took the hand of a lovely young woman. Her face was fair and well-proportioned—graceful brows, full lips, petite nose. Her hair, a similar color to Nathan's, was pinned up neatly into a tasteful coiffure. And she had a long, elegant neck that made her appear regal. There was no denying that she was exceptionally beautiful.

Though she held herself upright and poised, there was shyness in her expression as she looked at the entourage of people before her. Then, Nathan saw a flash of recognition and panic in her deep brown eyes. Following her line of sight, he turned around and saw a similar expression across Peter's face. His heart dropped. Understanding struck him with nauseating clarity.

He faced the woman again and saw that she had already recovered herself before anyone else took notice. She forced a pretty, gracious smile onto her face.

"Nathan," Daniel said. "I'd like to introduce you to my fiancée."

Sarah.

27

Sarah and the Hambletons convened in the parlor for tea. Nathan stood near the window, as far away from the group as he could without being suspicious, watching Sarah closely over the lip of his cup. She was demure, said very little, but listened to others with rapt attention and smiled often. She was the picture of beauty and affable complaisance, and Nathan hated her. Everything about her presence bothered him. Not only did she have Peter's heart, which made him sick with jealousy, but she was also a damned fortune hunter.

His mind raced. What if seeing Peter reignites old feelings in her and she tries to seduce him? What if Peter begs to have her back? His stomach lurched at the thought. Or, what if Peter couldn't bear to be near her and he was drafting his resignation letter at that very moment? Nathan did not want Peter to leave, but he also didn't want him to be working as Sarah's groundskeeper once she and Daniel had married. He decided that he had to speak with his mother and convince her to hire Peter on at the London home. Even if there wasn't much need for a groundskeeper, there was surely a need for another footman. Or perhaps a valet! Nathan's previous valet had resigned after the incident last autumn. Yes, Peter could make a very good valet, he thought. Although, it was an intimate job, and he suddenly worried that, given their conversation by the stream, it might cross a boundary.

As his thoughts ran in circles, he felt increasingly anxious and ill. Watching Sarah sit beside Daniel and their mother giggling lightly and easily, he thought for a moment that he might be physically sick. Daniel deserved to know the truth. Sarah had only pretended to love him. She really loved Peter and chose Daniel solely for his money. If Daniel knew the truth, he'd surely call off the wedding, and Sarah would be welcomed here no longer.

The thought immediately settled Nathan's nerves. If he could make Daniel realize that she was lying, many of his problems would be solved in an instant. Sarah would leave, Daniel would avoid a disastrous marriage, and the summer home would remain available for Nathan to continue living in. He wouldn't have to go back to London with his parents, and Peter could stay as the groundskeeper.

He considered his options. He could tell Daniel what Peter had told him, but that may lead to resentment against Peter. Or Daniel may be blinded by his own infatuation and could choose not to believe him, arguing that it is merely his word against hers. It would be better if Sarah told Daniel the truth herself, and Nathan thought that he might be able to convince her to do just that. A plan was coming together in his head. He just needed some time alone with her.

"Well," Nathan's mother said, rising to her feet. "I'd like to freshen up before dinner, and I'm sure you two would both like to settle into your rooms. Shall we all reconvene in the dining room?"

"An excellent idea, Mother," Daniel said, giving Sarah a hand off the couch. "Sarah, darling, I'll show you to your chambers."

Their mother gave Daniel a cross look. "You're not married *yet*. Mrs. Fairchild will show Sarah to her room." Daniel shot Nathan a small look of exasperation while their mother tugged on the nearby bell pull.

Jude appeared a moment later and everyone left, except for Nathan's father, who had said nothing since tea began, only sulked beside the mantle and watched the others converse with distaste. Nathan set down his teacup and began to leave, but when he passed by, his father reached out and grabbed his arm with surprising speed and strength.

"I'd like a word with you," he growled.

Nathan tried to pull his arm away, but his father's grip tightened hard enough to make him wince. He glanced at the door, wishing that someone—anyone—would come to his rescue.

His father yanked violently on his arm to pull Nathan's attention back. "Look at me when I speak to you. And listen well, because I'll not say it again." His eyes were dark and his jaw tight. "I have had it with your theatrics. I've tried to be patient."

Patient? Hot indignation began to burn inside Nathan. He has never exercised patience with him. Even when Nathan was a child, he was short-tempered. Nathan wanted to argue but held his tongue. He could feel that his father was dangerously close to expressing himself with violence.

"But I've had enough," his father continued. "I wanted you to follow in Daniel's footsteps and pursue business, but your mother insisted that you should be allowed to follow your interests. So, I let you study whatever useless drivel you wanted to in university—literature, poetry, art history. And I let you study as much as you wanted, too, for all the good that did! Then, I generously let you live in this house for months, in the hopes that you would eventually come to your senses, but you are as obstreperous as ever. I will *not* be making any further compromises, do you understand? One more misstep and I'll have you committed."

Nathan was mildly surprised to find that he was not afraid. His father's threats didn't frighten him in the least, because he felt a certainty in his core that he would never allow himself to go to an asylum. He would run away or take his own life before that happened. He realized in that moment that whatever power his father had over him, he was never truly helpless. He still had sway over his life.

With clenched teeth, his father leaned into Nathan's face, "Do I make myself clear?"

Nathan glared back at him, full of pride and defiance, then jerked his arm away from his father's grip with more force than he knew he had. His father started in surprise.

"Quite," Nathan said evenly and marched to the door. He could hear his father's rumble grow louder and more frustrated behind him, but he didn't follow him. One day, Nathan thought, that sound would bring the house down to rubble.

28

At dinner, Daniel and his mother did most of the talking, asking questions and leading the table from one topic to the next. Sarah smiled and spoke lightly on things, apparently preferring to listen. Probably because she was out of her depth and afraid of saying something that would expose herself as a fraud, Nathan thought. Besides that, passivity endeared her to her future mother-in-law who seemed well-pleased by her mild-mannered disposition. Watching his mother interact with Sarah, he saw how much she really did like her. It was evident that all of the vitriol from before and attempts at sabotaging the wedding had been purely his father's influence.

His father sat quietly, eating his dinner and pointedly avoiding eye contact with Sarah. She tried more than once to smile at him, but he was stubbornly looking away. Nathan could almost sympathize with her. Under different circumstances, he would be doing everything possible to make her feel welcome in spite of his father's coldness. In fact, Nathan bristled at the thought that he and his father shared a common interest in wanting Sarah gone. Still, he wouldn't let that deter him from his plan. It must be done for Daniel's sake, if nothing else. His brother was a good man, well-deserving of true love and happiness.

"Daniel, you have yet to tell me the story of how you and Sarah met," Nathan said warmly.

"Oh! How rude of me," Daniel said with a good-natured grin. "Our meeting was utter fortuity. One day, I came home early from the brokerage firm—something I almost never do—and behold, the most beautiful woman I've ever laid eyes on was in our house!" He smiled at Sarah, and she bashfully looked away concealing her own smile behind her napkin. "She was in for Mother, you see. Sarah is a seamstress. She had tailored a new dress for her.

And in fact, she was just leaving as I was entering, and we nearly collided. It was fate, I'm certain of it."

Their father grumbled something to himself, and Daniel purposefully ignored him. It was rather strange seeing them at odds. They normally got along very well. Their father had always been very proud of Daniel—for his handsome features, for his business savvy, for his career successes. Nathan never thought he would see the day that their father disapproved of him.

"The rest, as they say, is history," Daniel concluded.

"I think that's a most charming story." Nathan shifted his attention, "Sarah, you must forgive me my ignorance—I've been a bit removed from wedding talk. Will you be having any family or friends in attendance?"

Sarah looked at him solemnly. "I'm afraid not."

"No one?" he asked. "No parents or uncles or cousins? A younger brother, perhaps?"

At the mention of a younger brother, Sarah's eyes snapped to meet his. There was a sudden sharpness in her look as if trying to read him. Then, her face became docile once again, and she sighed sorrowfully, "No, I'm afraid not. I haven't any family to speak of."

Nathan had to stop himself from smiling. It was as he had hoped. She'd exposed her Achilles' heel, and he now had the leverage he needed to make her confess. "My goodness, how awful," he said sympathetically. "I'm very sorry to hear that."

The dreary topic made Nathan's mother restless in her seat, and she quickly interposed, "You know, Sarah, Nathaniel has become quite taken with botany as of late. In fact, he gave me a tour of the greenhouse yesterday, and his knowledge of different species is really most impressive."

"Nathan, is that true?" Daniel asked heartily.

"Yes, and believe me, I'm as surprised as you are. But I've truly found it most rewarding."

"Perhaps, Daniel and I could have a tour sometime as well," Sarah said politely.

Daniel beamed. "That's an excellent idea! Better yet, darling, I think the two of you should go without me. Nathan, I've been eager for you and Sarah to become better acquainted before the wedding. I feel it's only right that you should know your sister-in-law beforehand."

"I'd be more than happy to," Nathan said. "Sarah, I can show you the lake and gardens, as well."

"That sounds lovely," she said, her perfect smile wavering only slightly.

"Splendid," Daniel said. "Perhaps tomorrow afternoon? I'll be in the village to meet with the vicar regarding the wedding anyway."

"Tomorrow afternoon," Nathan agreed and gave Sarah a small smile over his wine glass.

———

"The grounds here are beautiful," Sarah said, keeping a leisurely pace beside Nathan as they walked along the path towards the gardens.

"They are, aren't they," Nathan said, a bit distractedly. He glanced toward the greenhouse to see if he could make out Peter's shape. Peter hadn't stopped by his room after closing the house last night. He wanted desperately to speak with him, to try to make amends with him however he could, to tell him that he wouldn't have to worry about Sarah for much longer. But he hadn't seen him since Daniel and Sarah's arrival.

"You know," he continued lightly. "These grounds have undergone a rather dramatic transformation in the past few months, thanks to our new groundskeeper. He's exceptional at his craft, and I must say, a rather wonderful teacher as well. He taught me everything I know about botany." Sarah said nothing, only stopped to admire a flowerbed. "Perhaps, you know him. His name is Peter."

She went very still for a moment, then turned to him with a cool, level expression. Her eyes had changed from soft and serene to sharp and focused. "Why would I know him?"

Nathan matched her stare, his blood beginning to boil. That she could not only break Peter's heart but also now pretend she didn't know him at all was loathsome. She was cold, callous, calculating, and finally going to face the consequences of her selfishness.

He decided to strike. "When do you plan to tell Daniel that you don't love him?"

Sarah looked thunderstruck, face turning red and struggling to find words. "Wh— You— I-I *beg* your pardon! I love Daniel very much!"

"Please, spare me the act," he said flatly. "You broke off your prior engagement solely for Daniel's money. You don't love him. You're nothing more than a fortune hunter."

She looked at him incredulously, mouth puckered. "Daniel is well aware that I don't come from money. You talk as if I sought him out and seduced him, but he pursued *me.*"

"And then, you let him believe that you loved him, which you don't."

"Another baseless accusation." She folded her arms smugly, "What proof have you that I don't love him?"

"Andrew," Nathan replied simply. Sarah paled. "You've hidden him from my family, which I can only assume is because he is the real reason you entertained Daniel's romantic interest at all. To tell him of your brother would be to reveal your true motivation. You care only about Andrew's wellbeing, nothing else. Admittedly, I can sympathize with your situation as I care very much for my own brother, also. That said, I will not stand idly by and watch him espouse a liar."

"And why should he believe you? If you tell him about Andrew, I'll only deny it."

"Quite right," he agreed. "That's why I think it would be best for you to tell him yourself."

She scoffed, "Not bloody likely."

"It would make things easier, but the truth will reveal itself either way, I assure you. There are investigators in London for hire who can find your brother. I don't imagine it would be difficult. Knowing what I do about his physical condition, I'm willing to bet that he shares a flat with you. It'd only be a matter of finding where you live in the city, which should be relatively short work given that I know your name and profession. So, either you can tell Daniel yourself, or we can involve Andrew directly. And sure, he can deny being your kin, but it won't help your situation. What would the world think of a young man living with a beautiful, unmarried woman out of wedlock? That would be quite a scandal."

Her face filled with outrage. "This is the problem with your lot! You throw money at anything to get your way. While the rest of us struggle to make enough money for the barest necessities. And God forbid, we should lose our ability to work and be condemned to the poor houses. Andrew never asked— It wasn't his *fault.* A-And he deserves—" Sarah's ire suddenly crumbled to pieces, revealing despair beneath it. She seated herself on the nearby bench and buried her head in her hands. Nathan felt a pang of sympathy and regret then but quickly steeled himself. It was likely nothing more than another performance.

When she lifted her head, her eyes were red and wet. "All right, fine. I'll admit that I let Daniel court me because I wanted to provide for Andrew. And I'll even admit that I didn't initially feel remorse for my decision to do so. But I'll not lie to Daniel and tell him I don't love him." She looked at Nathan with steadfastness. "He's a good man. A very good man, in fact—kind, warm, surprisingly humble. And he saw me as *somebody.* He's never once made me feel inferior to him. He's the son of a viscount, and I'm a seamstress for pity's sake. But he's shown me every respect, and over time, I fell in love. I didn't imagine I would, but I have. It isn't an act."

Nathan watched her closely. She seemed sincere, but still he stood his ground. "Even if you do love him, I have a hard time believing that's worth anything. You claimed to love Peter once, too."

"I still do love Peter," she said fiercely. "And I feel horrible for what I did to him. But Peter—" She sighed heavily. "Peter will be all right in the end. I have every confidence that he will find love and happiness without me someday. Andrew, however… Without me, he wouldn't have a life at all. And however much I may love another man, I will never love them more than I do my brother. He is the only family I have left, and I would die for him to live."

"Peter was prepared to give you everything you wanted!" he said exasperatedly. "He was willing to care for both you and Andrew. He went through great lengths to prove himself to you, but you still wanted more."

"It isn't so simple!" she protested. "The life of a farmer isn't a reliable one. If we suffered financially one year, Andrew would most certainly feel like a burden onto us and our resources. It wouldn't matter what I say to him."

Nathan laughed derisively. "Now I'm convinced that you never loved Peter at all! You go to such great lengths inventing reasons why life with him couldn't possibly work without even giving him a chance. What a grave injustice it is that he gave you his beautiful heart and you tossed it aside like nothing. You never deserved him."

Sarah watched him intently as he slowly calmed his heaving breaths, realization dawning in her eyes. An intrigued smile played on her lips. "My God…" she said with wonder. "You love him."

Nathan felt the blood drain from his face. "Don't be absurd," he spat.

"But you do," she said, grinning wickedly. "I can see it on your face when you talk about him. You *love* Peter, I can't believe it." She threw her head back and laughed.

"I do *not!* Peter is a good friend, nothing more. I care for him in the same way I do Daniel."

She ignored him. "It all makes perfect sense now. This confrontation had nothing to do with Daniel's happiness at all. You were compelled by your own envy and bitterness."

"That's a lie," Nathan snapped. "I want nothing but happiness for Daniel, and I doubt very much that he'd find it with someone like you."

Sarah stood from the bench and walked over to face him directly. "Does Peter know? No, I'm almost certain he doesn't. He would resign from his position if he knew the truth. He isn't *like* you."

Nathan held his tongue and didn't tell her that Peter had already learned the truth. Her words made him wonder though if Peter was, in fact, planning his resignation. Cold sweat broke on his forehead.

"What if I were to tell him?" she said sweetly. "How would you feel if your 'good friend' left this place because he learned that you loved him?"

"He wouldn't believe you," he said as calmly as he could. "Because there is no truth to it."

She looked at him with mock sympathy. "Peter and I have a long history together. I know him better than anyone, and he knows I'm a shrewd judge of character. He trusts me. Make no mistake, he'll believe me. However, I don't have to say anything. The choice is yours."

"You mean if I stay silent about Andrew."

"That's right. I was being honest before; I do love Daniel. But I worry that once he learns about Andrew after all this time, he may have doubts, questioning why I never told him before. And it's been hard enough to win the approval of your parents—well, your mother's approval, anyway—I don't want her opinion of me to lessen either."

Nathan considered his position. What did it matter if she told Peter about his feelings? He already knew. However, he had been holding onto the hope that he could make amends with him, but if Sarah intervened, that could be ruined. She could fill his head with lewd lies and convince him to leave. On the other hand, if Daniel didn't learn about Andrew now, his marriage would be founded on lies. And if at some point the truth of Andrew finally reached him—after he and Sarah had married and begun their family—he would be devastated by his wife's dishonesty. Nathan couldn't let that happen. He had a duty to his brother's happiness and well-being. It may cost him his relationship with Peter, but then again, he may have already ruined it anyway.

Though it felt like a knife in the heart, the answer was obvious. He took a slow breath and resigned himself to his future—a life without Peter.

"Tell Peter whatever you like," he told her. "So long as you tell Daniel the truth. And if you won't, I will."

Shock was plastered on her face. "I-I'll also tell your family! I'll tell them what you are. I can make Daniel believe me."

He sighed and shrugged, "I'm already a disappointment to them." Feeling suddenly tired, he rubbed a hand across his face. "You've built so much of your life on lies. Did it ever occur to you that telling Daniel the truth may not change anything? He loves you dearly. And you said it yourself—he's a good man. I only want what's best for him. So, if you really love Daniel, just tell him the truth. He deserves that and you know it."

Sarah looked at him, anxiously chewing on her lip, but said nothing.

Nathan turned to leave then stopped and shook his head. He didn't have the energy to harbor anymore resentment. "And I'm sorry. For before. I shouldn't have accused you of being a fortune hunter. I was being protective of my brother. I'm sure you can understand. For what it's worth, I hope it works out. For all of you. Andrew, too. You all deserve happiness." With that, he walked out of the garden back towards the house, leaving Sarah with her thoughts.

"Nathan!" she called out to him. He stopped to look at her. She was twisting her handkerchief nervously in her hands. "You don't think he'll hate me?"

He smiled to himself then. For the first time since meeting her, he could see with absolute certainty that, underneath all her defenses and masks, she did love Daniel. Perhaps, there was still hope for his brother's future yet.

"No," he said. "I don't think he will."

29

Nathan spent the rest of the afternoon in the conservatory away from the others with a book in his lap, barely pretending to read. He kept his gaze trained on the grounds, looking for any signs of Peter. Every hour that passed without seeing him made him increasingly anxious. He wanted more than anything to make amends with him as soon as possible. The world around him seemed off-kilter without Peter in it.

He felt confident that Sarah wouldn't mention his feelings for Peter. Not now. She was likely too preoccupied thinking of what she would say to Daniel. Nathan did hope that the conversation would go well for them both. He still detested how she had treated Peter in the past, but he could see that she and Daniel honestly loved each other. They had the chance to be truly happy.

As he sat basking in the sun rays pouring in from the windows, he wondered what he might say to Peter to repair their friendship. He could blame his isolation at the summer home for his abnormal romantic desires and claim that he was merely confused by the physical affection. He could insist that his anatomical impulses did not, in any way, reflect the thoughts of his rational mind. The body was an irrational, oftentimes inconsistent, instrument, especially so for him. His eyes saw things that no one else did, his ears heard conversations that no one else could. Yes, the body was an unreliable thing, indeed. Surely, Peter could understand that whatever effect he had on Nathan physically was no more real than his visions and nightmares.

This was all a lie of course. Nathan hated the idea of lying to Peter. But the truth was too dangerous. If a small, inconsequential lie could mend a precious friendship then surely it was worth it.

He sat up straighter in his chair as he saw movement outside. It was Peter, walking along the pathway towards the barn. Nathan jumped out of his chair and quickly made for the nearest exit, but just as he left the conservatory Jude hurried towards him. She was wringing her hands.

"Nathan—"

"Jude, it's good to see you, but I need to step outside and catch—"

"Nathan," she said more insistently. "Peter gave me his resignation letter." He stopped in his tracks. His heart sank to the floor. Jude looked at him dolefully. "I spoke with him just now. I knew I had to tell you right away. His last day is the day after next."

"Are you—?" He struggled to find his words. "What did he say? Did he mention why?"

Jude glanced around them briefly, aware that they were in a very public portion of the house. With a jerk of her head, she indicated for him to follow her, and they walked to his chambers. Once behind closed doors, she continued.

"He said that Daniel's fiancée Sarah was once *his* fiancée!" Astonishment was evident in her eyes. "Can you believe that? Needless to say, he couldn't bear to serve the house of the woman who broke his heart. I don't blame him in the slightest! Can you *imagine?* The poor man has unknowingly spent the past few months tirelessly preparing the grounds for his former fiancée's wedding!"

"Did he say anything else? Any other reasons for leaving?"

She clucked, "I'd say that is reason enough! I told him I understood his decision, and that I'd be happy to provide a strong reference should he need one." She looked thoughtful as she recalled the conversation. "And then, I mentioned you. I told him—I hope you don't mind me saying so—but I told him that I knew you would miss him terribly. And he said that he didn't think you would, which I found very odd. Everyone can see how well you two get along."

Nathan furrowed his brow. "He said that he didn't think that *I* would miss *him*?"

"That's right," she said. "Does this have anything to do with yesterday? I told you, he seemed upset even before Sarah arrived."

"Now I'm not sure." He sat down on his bed and put his elbows on his knees. Perhaps, Peter had said it to protect Nathan's secret. It seemed like him to protect someone else even amid his own hurt. "Though, I can't help but think I'm partly to blame for his leaving. You see, yesterday…" He took a breath and steadied himself. Though he trusted Jude completely, he still found it difficult to say the words aloud. "Yesterday, Peter learned my true feelings for him. He knows that I love him as more than a friend." Nathan felt his face immediately flush in embarrassment.

This news didn't seem surprising to her in the slightest, but she did seem somewhat confused. She narrowed her eyes at him, "And you're suggesting that's the reason he's chosen to leave?"

"Well, yes. I thought that was obvious."

She walked over to sit beside him on the bed and took his hands in hers. "Nathan, dear, guide me through the conversation. Did you actually *tell* Peter that you loved him?"

He was perplexed by this line of questioning and becoming a little annoyed. "Yes! Not in those exact words. But it couldn't have been more obvious. What are you getting at?"

"Forgive my saying so, but I get the feeling that you weren't as obvious as you imagined you were."

"What are you talking about?"

She sighed and said patiently, "I've seen the way you two get on. I've seen the way you both look at each other when the other's turned away. And the way you both talk about the other when they're not around. You both do it. You're like two children experiencing love for the first time and don't know how to say it yet."

"*Ridiculous*," Nathan pulled his hands away and stood from the bed. His heart began to race hopefully, but he quickly tempered his excitement with rationality. "You're looking for romance where there is none."

She stood then, too, and placed her hands firmly on her hips. "You're not the only one with keen insights, you know. In fact, for as much as you see in the world around you, there's a fair bit that you don't."

"Jude, when he learned the truth about my feelings, he *left*. He ran away and hasn't spoken to me since."

"Was it a declaration of love, or did you let implication speak for you?"

He opened his mouth to retort, then stopped. It certainly hadn't been a declaration, but surely the truth had been clear. Though, what if it hadn't been? Doubt began to set in. "I-I'm certain he understood. My meaning was more than obvious."

She folded her arms then with a satisfied look on her face. "I'll assume that means the latter."

"You think we're both operating under a misunderstanding?"

"I'd put money on it. I think you should tell him how you feel plainly, without any possibility for confusion."

"What good would that do? I've already subjected him to the topic once. And regardless, he'll likely still leave because of Sarah anyway."

"I can't say if it *will* do any good or change anything, but it very well might. That's the thing about uncertainty, isn't it? There's always the possibility of something greater, and if you don't at least try, you may wonder for the rest of your days about what could've been. And as I see it, you've nothing left to lose. He's already planning to leave. Wouldn't you rather live your life knowing that you were completely honest with him?"

He ruminated on her words. Not ten minutes before, he'd been prepared to lie to save his friendship with Peter, but now he couldn't bring himself to it. It didn't feel right. After all, he berated Sarah for her lies and pressured her to tell Daniel the truth. To lie now would make him a hypocrite. Daniel deserved honesty and so, too, did Peter.

"Since yesterday," he said, "I've desperately wanted to talk with him to try to mend things. But if he is leaving, I suppose you're right that I have nothing to lose by telling him the truth. At the very least, it would be worth it just to see him again, one last time."

Jude reached out and took his hand again. She smiled, gave him a small squeeze, and said, "Good luck."

30

That evening, Nathan sat at the dinner table with a letter he'd written to Peter burning a hole in his jacket pocket. Not having much of an appetite, he pushed the food around his plate absently, feeling a mix of eagerness and apprehension at the thought of delivering it. He wondered what change, if any, it may have on things to come. The most he could hope for was understanding. He realized after talking with Jude that, more than anything else, he wanted Peter to know—truly know—the nature of his feelings. That they weren't depraved or obscene. That they weren't cheap and common. That deep in his heart, he wanted every happiness for him.

Across the table, Sarah seemed nervous, too, as she was talking more than normal. Nathan interpreted this to mean that she hadn't yet spoken with Daniel about Andrew but that she planned to soon. Daniel, completely unsuspecting, was pleased to see her being so talkative and comfortable with his family and attributed it to her getting to know Nathan better.

"Darling, how was your outing with Nathan today?" he asked her.

"Oh, it was very inspiring," she said, and smiled at Nathan. He smiled back. There didn't appear to be any lingering hostility between them, which he was grateful for. Upon first seeing Nathan in the dining room, she nodded to him respectfully, and he did the same. There was a strange sense of understanding he felt they shared since their conversation in the garden. "Though, we never made it beyond the tour of the grounds. It was all I had the energy for today. There is so much to see!"

"There certainly is," Nathan agreed. "There is a fair bit more beyond the perimeter as well, if you and Daniel are ever in the mood for a longer walk someday."

"Nathaniel, darling, have you been exploring much beyond the estate since you've been here?" his mother asked curiously.

"Some. I never realized there was such a beautiful countryside beyond those hedges."

"I must admit," Sarah said, "having been raised in the country myself, it does feel refreshing to be away from the city. Nathan, I heard that you will be returning to London later this summer. Are you looking forward to it?"

He smiled ruefully. "It's been a long time away, but I'm sure I'll adjust to city life again quickly."

"Well, you're welcome to visit us here anytime, of course," she said, "but I imagine that Lord and Lady Hambleton will be happy to have you back."

A tense silence fell over the table, and Sarah looked around in wide-eyed alarm. Daniel and his mother stared at their plates. His father had remained quiet for the entire meal thus far, as was usual, but Nathan could hear his rumble growing louder and more frustrated.

"I'm terribly sorry, have I said something?" Sarah asked anxiously. "I was told that Nathan was here for his health, and he seems to be very well at the moment. Or, perhaps, I've misunderstood…" Her voice trailed off.

Nathan's mother chimed in with too much cheeriness in her voice, "Yes, that's exactly right! There's no need to apologize, dear. Nathaniel is doing much better, and yes, we are thrilled to have him home again. Isn't that right, Victor?"

His father gave her an irritated look, then turned to Sarah. "To be perfectly honest, these past eight months without him have been the most pleasant in recent memory."

Daniel and his mother spoke in unison:

"*Father!*"

"*Victor!*"

Nathan's cheeks burned, but he said nothing. He'd long since accepted his father's dislike of him, but still felt a deep resentment. He wanted to spit vitriol back at him but held his tongue. It wasn't worth his energy. Dinner would be over soon enough. He only cared about Peter, and the letter in his pocket.

Sarah laughed awkwardly. "Surely, your lordship jests."

He glowered at her. "No, I'm quite serious. If I had known my second son would've been such a disappointment, I would've been content to have only the first."

"Father, stop this," Daniel said hotly.

"Victor, you don't mean that! Apologize to Nathaniel at once!" his mother said crossly.

Sarah stared at Lord Hambleton, appalled.

"Damnit, I will *not*," he slammed a fist down onto the table, rattling the silverware. "I'll not put on a hollow show of cordiality for everyone else's comfort. It will not change the truth of the matter."

"Utterly *deplorable!*" Sarah said sharply. The table fell silent again. Daniel and his mother gaped at her. Nathan watched in amazement.

His father was stunned for only a moment. "I beg your pardon?" He said tightly, a dark warning in his voice.

She was unshaken. "Your behavior is utterly deplorable. I could never imagine a father saying such odious things to his son. And at dinner, no less, in the company of ladies! Your behavior is disgraceful. Have you any manners at all? Any decency? You are no gentleman, Lord Hambleton, and you should frankly be ashamed."

The rumbling emanating from him had grown violently loud and unsteady. It was a sound like heavy thunder and monolithic boulders colliding together, splitting.

"You'll excuse me. I've lost my appetite," Sarah said, rising from the table and setting her napkin down. She stared daggers at him, her unflinching eyes full of contempt.

Daniel jumped to his feet then and took her hand. He cleared his throat, "I couldn't agree more, darling. Let's retire to the parlor. Anyone interested in a brandy and *proper decorum* may join us." With that, he escorted her out.

Nathan's mother stood next. She didn't say anything, only looked at her husband disapprovingly and then held out a hand to Nathan. He rose from his seat and took her arm.

"Let's go, my darling," she said to him, and they both left Nathan's father behind in the dining room alone. His hands were balled into white fists, his nostrils flared. Nathan could hear his teeth grinding together over the sound of the thunder.

Outside of the dining room, his mother was silent, but rubbed a gentle hand over his forearm as they walked to the parlor. Sarah and Daniel were both happy to see them. Daniel poured them glasses of brandy and stayed very close to Sarah, beaming slightly. Nathan thought he looked proud.

Sarah caught Nathan's eye and subtly raised her glass to him from across the room. They shared a small, acknowledging smile. Perhaps, he thought, Sarah was just what his family needed after all.

"I'm very sorry, Sarah," Nathan's mother said. "My husband's behavior was inexcusable."

"I do appreciate you saying so," Sarah said. "Though, I can't help but worry… If that is how he speaks to his own son, might I someday be subjected to similar disrespect?"

"Never," Daniel said firmly. "I wouldn't allow that."

His mother raised her brandy, "Nor would I."

They drank and chatted easily amongst themselves for a while, leaving dinner behind them. Nathan did not stay long, however. He still had a mission to complete. Fortunately, no one protested when he excused himself to retire early.

He exited the parlor and quietly made his way through the house. He did not see any sign of his father; the dining room appeared to be emptied and cleaned when he passed by. He must have gone to bed, he thought. Still, Nathan moved cautiously. In the servants' quarters, he made his way down the hallway and approached the last room on the left. Peter's room. There was no light coming from beneath the door. He was likely still having dinner of his own with the rest of the staff, but Nathan wasted no time. He removed the letter from his pocket, slid it under the door, and returned to his chambers.

Now, he only had to wait.

31

Nathan paced nervously in the greenhouse. The moon was full and shone brightly through the glass, making everything as visible as day. He checked his pocket watch. It was five minutes until midnight now, and Peter should be arriving at any moment. Nathan felt confident that he would appear because he found the servants' entrance unlocked after the house had been closed for the night, per his instructions in the letter he slid under Peter's bedroom door. He'd clearly seen the message and agreed to play along, much to Nathan's relief. He wasn't sure what his plan would've been if Peter had ignored him.

The anticipation now was nearly unbearable. Nathan's palms were sweating, and his heart was thudding anxiously. The sweet, floral scent of late-season violets did nothing to calm his nerves. He didn't know exactly how things would turn out tonight, but he tried to have faith that, if nothing else, Peter would better understand him and his feelings.

He heard the greenhouse door open behind him and turned to see Peter stepping in. Even from where Nathan stood, he could see the tired look in his eyes. Peter stayed near to the door, shoulders visibly tight with discomfort. Nathan was overjoyed to see him again. He wanted nothing more than to run and embrace him.

Instead, he cleared his throat and asked, "How are you?"

Peter looked down at his feet and shrugged. "I've been better. What's this about?"

"I heard you were resigning."

"Yes, I think it's time that I moved on to the next thing. Whatever that may be."

"I understand." He swallowed around the lump in his throat. "I'll miss you."

Peter shook his head. "Please, don't."

Nathan's heart clenched painfully, and he considered abandoning his plans. His optimism from before was now nowhere to be found. But, if this was the last time he would ever speak to Peter, he thought, he had to make it count. He had to express the truth, for his own sake.

"A while ago, you asked me to play for you," he said, trying to sound as friendly as he could manage. He turned and retrieved his violin and bow from the bench behind him. "And I suppose it's now or never."

Peter said nothing, only folded his arms and watched him with skeptic curiosity as Nathan placed the violin beneath his chin. He positioned the bow and then closed his eyes. He hadn't practiced beforehand; he knew he didn't need to. The song he wanted Peter to hear would pour from him automatically, compulsively. He took a deep breath, let his fingers fall naturally on the fingerboard, and gently pushed his bow along the first string.

The song emerged eagerly, a melody that felt both new and familiar. It sounded like being young, like the healing warmth of spring, like treasure hunting in flowerbeds, like picnicking on sunny days, like sleeping in the hayloft. It sounded like unabashed laughter and tender embraces, like careful hands brushing away tears, like sleeping breaths synchronizing. It sounded like waking up in the morning and kissing your best friend, feeling the smile on their lips pressed against yours. It sounded like the song Nathan hummed unknowingly when he was with Peter. It sounded like love—the song in his heart.

Playing the piece, Nathan was spellbound by the outpouring of emotion. He was able to recall in vivid detail his fondest moments with Peter and felt enveloped in his presence. For that brief moment in time, it felt that nothing else in the world existed besides the two of them.

Finally, the song swelled to its final crescendo and then quieted. He slowly returned to the present and opened his eyes. Peter was standing closer than before, arms hanging at his sides, eyes open wide, tears streaming down his cheeks. At the sight of him, the air left Nathan's lungs.

"You— That song—" Peter faltered. His eyebrows furrowed in confusion. "You said that day, in the hayloft, that you had never been in love."

"I hadn't. That is, not before you. But at the time, I didn't understand that yet."

He shook his head. "All this time, I thought— I tried everything to keep my emotions controlled around you. To convince myself they weren't there at all."

Nathan's heart thudded wildly, and he let his violin and bow fall from his hands to the ground. "Does that mean…?" They both took a step toward each other.

"But then, what about before? By the stream? I thought I felt something between us, but then you recoiled from my touch. And said you didn't want our friendship to be ruined."

"Because my feelings for you are overwhelming, and I worried your touch would give me away. I didn't know that you felt the same. You… You do feel the same, don't you?"

They took another step toward each other, the remaining space between them becoming small and intimate. Nathan stared deeply into his kind blue eyes, captivated. They were no less brilliant in the moonlight. Their faces were close, and Nathan felt himself flushing hotly.

Peter stared back, tears still brimming in his eyes. Without warning, he took another small step forward, cupped his strong hands on the sides of Nathan's face, and brought their mouths together. Surprised, Nathan gasped and saw a dazzling starburst of color in his vision, as if looking through the kaleidoscope. Peter's warm, full lips fit naturally with his, and he melted against them. His eyes fluttered closed.

Then, after a moment that wasn't nearly long enough, Peter pulled away. Nathan's senses were completely filled with Peter, and he desperately wanted more. He felt dizzy and was trembling from head to toe. Peter took notice and rubbed his arms gently.

"Are you all right?" he asked, concerned.

Without a word, Nathan kissed Peter back in earnest. He slid his hands up to his strong chest, and Peter wrapped his arms around Nathan's waist. They kissed desperately, as if the other's lips had saved them from the brink of death. Their mouths moved together in harmony. Peter parted his lips, and Nathan followed, humming blissfully as Peter's tongue found his. Their tongues danced together, exploring tentatively, sliding past one another, and brushing against lips. It was unlike anything Nathan had ever known. It was exhilarating. It was intoxicating. It was an expression of everything he felt but couldn't convey with words or even music. It was perfect. It was Peter. He never wanted it to end. He could spend a lifetime kissing Peter and it still wouldn't be enough.

Despite both of their reluctance, they eventually stopped to catch their breath. Nathan rested his arms on Peter's shoulders, and Peter still had his wrapped securely around Nathan's waist. They took steadying breaths together and smiled. Nathan couldn't contain his happiness and a laugh escaped him. Peter laughed, too. Then, they rested their foreheads together and closed their eyes. In the middle of the greenhouse, surrounded by the garden they had cared for together, they swayed back and forth in each other's arms, relishing their private moonlit dance amongst the violets.

Nathan was so unbelievably happy—happier than he'd ever been in his life—but there was also a sadness in him. A sadness for his younger self who spent his entire life questioning his worthiness for love and affection, who wouldn't even let himself hope for companionship because he wouldn't be able to stand the disappointment. Hot tears fell from his eyes, and he buried his face in Peter's neck. Peter held him tighter, rubbing a soothing hand over his back. Nathan didn't feel embarrassed. Not with Peter. He knew he was safe with him, safer than he had ever felt in his own childhood home. And it occurred to him then, that when he was with Peter, he *was* home. Together, they made something beautiful and safe and tender—they made something that he had wanted for as long as he could remember.

After Nathan's tears had dried, they stayed holding each other. Breathing together. Simply being together. They stayed like that for a long time until Peter gently pulled away, and without a word, took Nathan's hand and led him out of the greenhouse. Nathan didn't care that he'd left his violin behind. It could wait.

Back inside the house, Peter locked the servants' entrance, and they walked quietly to his room at the end of the hallway. Nathan stepped in first and lit a small candle on the desk, while Peter, again, locked the door behind them. They removed their shoes and crawled into the bed. It was small, but neither seemed to mind.

They laid on their sides, silently looking at each other. Peter idly caressed Nathan's face. Nathan leaned forward and gently kissed him, a small, lazy brush on the lips. It was late and they were both tired. Nathan was vaguely aware that he should probably return to his own room, but the idea of sleeping beside Peter was too alluring. He knew if he closed his eyes, it would only be a matter of seconds before the need for sleep overtook him.

Peter spoke in a groggy whisper, "What will happen now? Neither of us is staying here."

Nathan suddenly remembered that tomorrow was Peter's last day at the summer home. He'd completely forgotten about Sarah and Daniel and their impending wedding. He'd forgotten about returning to London with his parents.

"Would you want to live with us in London? I'm certain I can convince my mother. There isn't much gardening to be done, but I do need a valet."

Peter gave him a sad smile. "I don't think I can stand to be around your father. Not after knowing how he treats you. Besides, as much as I enjoy the idea of watching you dress, I don't want the world to see me as your lowly servant."

Nathan blushed at the comment about watching him dress. "I understand. I don't want that either honestly. I just know that I want to see you every day of my life."

"I want that, too."

"What if you worked in London instead? You could have a place of your own, and I'd visit as often as possible."

"Maybe," he said, but he sounded doubtful even in his drowsy state. "I… I can't stay in London forever. But, maybe for a time I could…"

Nathan took Peter's hand in his own, "Let's try. And if you must leave the city someday, then I will find a way to follow."

He brought Nathan's hand to his lips and kissed his fingers. "All right. Let's try."

Nathan closed his eyes and sighed contentedly. He was filled to the brim with pure joy. There was a thought in the back of his mind that he must be dreaming, but he knew he wasn't. Tonight was everything that he wanted and more. He and Peter were together. And though the future wasn't precisely clear, they would weather the uncertainty, hand-in-hand.

Peter sat up to blow out the candle and then settled back into bed. He placed a small kiss on Nathan's forehead. "Goodnight, Nathan."

Fading fast, Nathan mumbled back, "Goodnight, Peter." And then, after a moment, "I love you." He felt Peter shift closer to him and place an arm around him.

"I love you, too."

32

Early in the morning, just as the thin light of dawn began to brighten Peter's small room, there came a knock at the door.

"*Six o' clock,*" Jude's voice called from the other side.

Peter stirred and called back, "Thank you, Mrs. Fairchild." He laid his head back down on the pillow and gently ran a hand through Nathan's hair.

Nathan opened his eyes tiredly, saw Peter, and grinned. "So, it wasn't a dream."

Peter smiled back and kissed him. "I wish we could spend all day like this."

Nathan yawned and rubbed the sleep from his eyes. "I'm embarrassed to admit that I didn't think this far ahead last night. Would it be safe to creep back to my chambers now?"

"No, not yet," Peter said, standing now and lighting the lamp on his desk. "But we'll all be having breakfast soon, and that's your chance. When I leave, stay put for another five minutes, and then it should be safe."

"Yes, sir." He watched from the bed as Peter began removing his clothes from the night before to put on a fresh set. Even now, some part of him still felt shy about watching, but given the circumstances, he supposed it was all right.

Peter unbuttoned his undergarments and let them fall to the floor, revealing his strong shoulders and backside. He was gorgeous, the most beautiful thing Nathan had ever seen. He wanted to run his hands over every inch of him, and he thought, someday, he may very well get his wish. The idea alone was enough to arouse him.

Fully bare, Peter glanced back over his shoulder at him and raised a suggestive brow. "I thought I felt eyes on me."

Before he could stop himself, he asked him, "Would you like to feel more than just eyes?" He immediately blushed in embarrassment and put his hands over his face. "My God, I'm terribly sorry. That was tasteless."

Peter laughed and pulled his hands away from his face. He was leaning over him and staring into his eyes from mere inches away. "To answer your question—Yes, I would. Very much." He moved forward and pressed a deep, longing kiss onto Nathan's lips. "But it will have to wait."

Nathan stared back into his perfect blue eyes and swallowed. From the corner of his vision, he could see Peter's own body rousing with excitement, but he wouldn't let himself look. Peter smiled down at him, kissed him briefly again, and then turned away to finish dressing.

"Remember, give it five minutes after I leave." He reached for the door handle, then stopped, and looked affectionately at Nathan. "If you have time, come find me later. Maybe we could revisit the hayloft." He gave him a wink and then disappeared into the hall.

Alone, Nathan fished out his pocket watch and checked the time. *Five minutes.* He laid in bed, pulled the blankets up to his nose, and breathed Peter in. It felt absurd to admit, but he already missed him.

He listened to the pattering of rain outside of the bedroom's small window and thought of the nap they took in the hayloft after their picnic. It seemed ridiculous in hindsight that he hadn't realized his own feelings for Peter at that time, even though they were certainly already present. Regardless, the thought of returning to the barn with Peter now made him smile. He could imagine curling up with him in a bed of hay and listening to the rain together. Talking and laughing and kissing and…

He glanced down at his watch. It was time to move.

———

Nathan had made it back to his chambers without detection. He changed into his nightshirt, crawled into bed, and slept for another hour or so before Jude knocked on his door.

"Good morning," she said, drawing back the curtains to reveal the grey, wet day outside. "I told William I'd fill in for him this morning."

Upon waking, Nathan noticed that the house seemed unusually serene, more than it had been in over a week. The rumbling was no longer there.

"Is Father gone?"

"He is, how did you know?" She looked at him, puzzled, then shook her head indifferently, "Never mind. Yes, your father left for the village about half an hour ago. Not sure for what exactly. But he certainly still seemed tense after last night."

"I take it word has spread to the staff about Sarah scolding him."

"Of course!" she said. "I can hardly believe she had the pluck! Though—and this is strictly between us—I'm glad she did. He shouldn't have said those things about you."

"Thank you. I'm glad she did, too. I really think she might be good for this family."

"Let's hope so." She sat down on his bed, "Now, tell me, how did things go last night? Did you speak with Peter?"

He wanted to keep a stoic face and keep her in suspense, but he was unable to stop himself from smiling. Jude's eyes went wide and excited.

"You mean—?" She was grinning now, too.

Nathan flopped back onto his pillows dramatically and draped his arms over his face, "Yes!"

Jude gasped animatedly. "Oh, Nathan, that's wonderful! And forgive me for being a nightmare, but *I told you so!*"

"No, you have every right," he laughed. "I should've never doubted you. It was so…*wonderful!* We spent hours together. In fact, I slept in his room last night."

She looked at him incredulously, her mouth a perfect circle. "*Nathaniel!* Do you mean to tell me that you were in his room when I woke him this morning?" He grinned mischievously at her, and she swatted at him. "Your *parents* are here! That's a risky game to play!"

"I know, I know. We won't make a habit of it."

"Well, I suppose that's true. He leaves tomorrow after all. What will you both do?"

"He's going back to London to look for work and a place of his own. We'll see each other as often as possible. Lord knows, I'll be eager to leave the house as much as I can anyway." He looked down at his hands. "I'll admit, though, I'm a little frustrated. All this time, Peter and I secretly felt the same about each other and didn't know it. If we had only realized it sooner, we could've had months here at the summer home together without any worry about my father at all. It would've been lovely."

She patted a comforting hand on the blanket where his shin was. "All that matters is that you both know now. You'll figure out a way to make it work in London. I have every confidence in you two."

"Thanks, Jude." He supposed she was right, but he knew it was going to be a challenge in the city. There would be many more eyes on them both. They would need to be very careful. And Nathan would have to find a way to live without Jude, too.

"Of course. Now, let's get you down to breakfast."

33

"Where's Father this morning?" Nathan asked his mother at the table.

She buttered her toast primly and replied, "I told him last night that if he couldn't be civil this morning, then he'd best make himself scarce. So, naturally, he's in the village today." Sarah and Daniel exchanged an approving look. "Your father has always had a stubborn temper, but it will settle in time. He will be back by lunch, I'm sure."

They all continued their breakfast, making easy conversation. It was nice, Nathan reflected, being with the three of them and not feeling the looming presence of his father. He noticed the air between Sarah and Daniel had shifted slightly from the night before. They both seemed more comfortable together, Sarah especially. Nathan wondered if it was because she had finally told him the truth about Andrew. He hoped so.

"I was wanting to tour the grounds again today, but this weather is dreadful," Sarah said. "I thought the land between the gardens and lake would be a beautiful spot for the reception, but I wanted to get a better look. Hopefully, the rain stops."

"I think that would be an excellent location, darling," Daniel agreed. "Perhaps, tomorrow will be better for going out. If so, it would be wonderful to finally see that greenhouse of yours, Nathan. If you'd care to show us, that is."

"I'd be delighted," he smiled.

After breakfast, the four of them parted ways, and Nathan settled into an armchair in the conservatory, looking through the wet windows for signs of Peter and considering the different ways he might be able to escape to the hayloft.

As he sat there daydreaming, a sudden wave of nausea washed over him, stirring him from his thoughts. It seemed that breakfast wasn't settling well. He stood from his chair to go to the lavatory when he was struck by an immense pain in his chest. It radiated from the left side of his body, through to his back, and down his arm. The blinding pain stopped him in his tracks, and he doubled over feeling as though he might be sick at any moment. He managed to shuffle to the bell pull and tug on it once before the terrible ache became too great and his legs buckled beneath him.

Sprawled out on the carpet, Nathan clamped a hand over his heart and stared vacantly at the ceiling above. He was dying. He felt it in his bones. Terror and confusion completely filled his mind.

Footsteps approached from outside the door, followed by a loud cry. "*Nathan!*" Jude kneeled down beside him. "Nathan, what's wrong? What is it?"

He couldn't speak. He couldn't breathe. His lungs wouldn't take air.

"Oh, dear God, you're turning blue!" she said, horrified. "I'll send someone for Doctor Beverley right away." She turned and called out loudly over her shoulder, "*WILLIAM! WILLIAM!*"

All at once, as quickly as it had come, the pain left Nathan's chest and his lungs opened again. He gasped desperately for air as if he'd been submerged underwater, and as he did, a terrible realization came into his consciousness like a bolt of lightning. Jude put an arm around his shoulders and helped him sit upright.

"Nathan! Are you all right? What happened? *WILLIAM! Where are you!?*"

"No… No doctor," he heaved, waving a hand at her. "I need… Peter. It's… It's his father." He scrambled to his feet and clumsily ran through the house, bumping against thresholds and pushing off of walls.

Jude was hot on his heels. "Peter's father?"

"He's— He's sick."

By the time he reached the exit in the servants' quarters, he had regained most of his composure and bolted from the door, running as fast as his legs could carry him to the greenhouse. He knew Peter would be there. The rain was coming down hard now, but he barely noticed. His heart and thoughts were racing.

When he reached the greenhouse, he threw the door open. Peter turned and looked surprised to see him.

"Nathan! You forgot your violin last—" He stopped when he saw his face.

"I'm so sorry, Peter," he sobbed; he couldn't remember when he started crying. "It's your father. He's— I think he might be— He isn't well. You have to go."

Peter's face went deathly pale, and he dropped the clippers he was holding. "You mean he's…?"

Nathan stepped urgently toward him and grabbed his hand, "I won't say for certain. There might still be time, I don't know. But you must go, now!"

Together they ran back to the house through the downpour. The servants' entrance was open, and Jude was standing just inside talking with Sarah, Daniel, and Nathan's mother. The three of them looked from Nathan to Peter to Jude in utter bewilderment. They must have heard the commotion from before when Nathan had collapsed in the conservatory. Peter stepped into the house and walked past them all without a word and made for his room down the hall.

"Master Nathan," Jude said nervously. "I was just telling everyone how we received a *telegram* with the terrible news about Peter's father."

He cleared his throat. "Yes, that's right. He's in very poor health. I'm not sure he has much time."

Sarah put a hand over her mouth.

"The poor man," his mother said solemnly. "Mrs. Fairchild, please arrange for a carriage to take Peter directly to the train station in the next town. Nathaniel, dear, you were very courageous, running through the rain and all! Now come darling, let's get you dried off."

"One moment, Mother. I'd like to say goodbye to Peter and give him my condolences. He's a very good friend."

"Oh!" She blinked in mild surprise. "Of course! We'll give you two privacy. But please do change your clothes right after. I don't want you to catch a cold."

Nathan walked down the hall and stepped into Peter's room, closing the door behind him. Peter, who was frantically packing his things into his trunk, stopped when he entered. His eyes were red and swollen. He dropped the fistful of clothes in his hands to the floor and closed the gap between them, crashing hard into Nathan. He buried his face into his neck and sobbed. Nathan wrapped his arms tightly around him and rubbed a hand tenderly on his back.

"I should've been there," Peter said hoarsely. "I should've been there."

"You couldn't have known. Nobody could've." Nathan held him for several minutes, listening to the heartbreaking sounds of Peter's cries and the heavy patter of rain. He wished there was something, anything he could do to ease his hurt. But he knew there was nothing. All he could do was be there for him and show him love. They slowly rocked back and forth on their feet, as if rocking themselves to sleep. He could've held him like that for hours, but there came a knock at the door.

Jude stuck her head inside, "There's a carriage waiting for you, Peter. Whenever you're ready."

"Right," he said, pulling away from Nathan and wiping his nose. "Of course. I'll be there soon."

When Jude left, Peter continued stuffing clothes and shoes into his trunk, and Nathan helped. They moved together in silence, finding comfort in just each other's company. As they were nearly finished, they glanced around the room looking for anything they may have forgotten.

Peter's eyes found Nathan's. His face was despondent. "I can't go to London—"

"I know," He assured him. "And I wouldn't ask you to."

"But I can't do this without you, Nathan. I need you with me."

He wiped a tear from Peter's cheek. He had a realization before—when he was running through the rain to the greenhouse—that it would come to this. He'd made up his mind at that very moment what he was going to do.

"I'm going with you," he smiled. It would be challenging, he knew, to leave his mother and Jude behind and to adjust to life on a farm. It would also be a painful journey for Peter as he navigates his grief. But he was prepared to face all of it. After everything he and Peter had endured together over the past months, there wasn't anything they couldn't handle.

"You are?" Peter looked amazed. "You'd do that? Give up your life for me?"

"In a heartbeat. I can't imagine a life that I would want more than one spent with you."

Peter kissed him then without warning and surprised them both. He let out a wet laugh, "You really are a wonder."

Nathan blushed and pressed a small kiss on the corner of his mouth. "I wish I could make the trip with you now, but I need to say goodbye first to my mother and Daniel. I won't be long behind you."

"Of course, I understand." Peter turned to rummage through his desk drawer, removed an envelope, and handed it to Nathan. It was empty but an address had already been printed on the front. "I was planning to send them money again, like I do every month. This is the address."

"We'll be together again soon," Nathan promised.

34

Nathan waved at Peter's carriage as it disappeared down the long road leading to the manor. Once it was out of sight, he sprang into action and went to his chambers to pack. He did not want to waste any time. Seeing as his father was still in the village, it was as opportune a time as any. It would be best if his father didn't learn about his departure until after he was already gone.

In his room, he grabbed his trunk and began packing away clothes and books and sentimental tokens he wanted to take with him. He set aside the biscuit tin from the greenhouse to give to Daniel later.

When he was nearly finished, there was a quiet knock at the door. "Come in, Jude," he called out.

She stepped inside quickly and shut the door behind her, looking around at the room and the trunk that Nathan was filling. "I thought you might be leaving. Have you told your mother?"

"No, not yet. I will after I'm finished here. I'll tell Daniel, too."

"I'll miss you, you know." Nathan looked up at her then. She gave him a sad smile, "You really are a wonderful friend."

He walked over to her and pulled her into a hug. "I'll miss you, too. But this isn't goodbye. I know it might feel like it, but we'll see each other again someday. I'm certain of it." He wasn't saying that simply to be pleasant; he truly meant it.

She nodded and wiped her eyes. "I'm sure you're right." He could hear the doubt in her voice. "You'd better get a move on before your father finds out."

"That's my intention. He took the other carriage into town with him, I assume?"

"Yes, that's right. Let's hope Peter's carriage returns before your father does."

He shut the lid of the trunk and fastened the straps. "Please, be on the watch for it. Have the footman load my trunk as soon as it arrives, and then come find me. By then, I will hopefully be finished saying my goodbyes."

—

Nathan knocked on his mother's door.

"*Come in!*" she sang out.

Upon entering, he found his mother sitting at her dressing table applying fresh powder on her cheeks. Her lady's maid stood behind her, tidying her hair with pins.

"Oh! Come in, darling. I was just freshening up before tea. Thank you, Eliza, that's all for now." Her lady's maid slipped past Nathan and shut the door on her way out. "Did you see your friend off, dear? I do hope his father is all right."

"Yes, Peter's gone," he said. "And I'm leaving, too."

She stopped primping in the mirror and turned to him, confused. "Leave? Now? Darling, what do you mean?" She walked over to him and led him by the hand to the bed to sit with her. "What's this about?"

"Mother, I'm going to live with Peter. He's a very good friend and he needs me." He swallowed. "And I need him."

She stared at him for a long while as if seeing him for the first time, a look of wonder on her face. "You and Peter…?"

"Yes, that's right." He held a steady, composed expression, trying not to reveal his anxiousness.

"I should've known," she said to herself and gave him a sad smile. "I said before that you seemed different. You're happier. More vibrant. I should've known it was love. I'm your mother, I should've realized it sooner."

"You're not angry?"

"Nathaniel, how could I be? It's as you said before with Daniel and Sarah. They love each other and they're happy. What more could I want as a mother?"

"Grandchildren?" he grimaced.

She threw back her head and laughed. "I'll admit, if I wasn't expecting them from Daniel over the next few years, that might've been a greater concern. You should probably thank him for that." Nathan laughed now, too.

"Darling," she continued. "I want you to be happy. And I know living in London again, with your father... Well, I know you'd hate it. And as much as I want you back at home, I couldn't stand to see you miserable. Also, as of late, I worry that it wouldn't be safe for you..." She looked down and fidgeted with her bracelet. "Just— Please don't stop being my son. Never stop writing. Promise me that."

"Mother, of course," he placed his hands over hers. "I would never. I know how much family means to you. And please know, I plan to see you however I can. It may be a challenge, but there must be some way to make it happen. Maybe private visits in the city when Father is out for the day. Or you could spend a few days with us out in the country if you'd like."

"I'd like that very much." She tried to smile, but it fell short. "Your father is going to be furious when he finds out, you know. I think it would be best if you were to leave before he returns."

"I will. I've already packed. I'm only waiting for Peter's carriage to return."

A thought seemed to strike her. "Oh! But what on earth will you do for money, darling? Do you have any? Your father's money will certainly be out of the question from here onward."

"I have what's in my pockets," he told her. "It should be more than enough to make the journey."

"And what about Peter? Does he have any money?"

"I'm not sure. He comes from a farming family."

His mother seemed to think on this for a moment before she began pulling the rings from her fingers one by one, save for her wedding band.

"Mother, no, I couldn't," Nathan protested, but she placed the rings in his hands and then began removing her earrings next.

"I'll not hear it," she told him firmly. Once she'd removed all of the gold and precious stones from her person, she walked over to the dressing table and retrieved her jewelry box. It was filled with her favorite pieces. "Take it. It's worth more than this house, I'm sure."

"Mother, thank you, but I simply won't," he insisted.

"Really, it's fine. I have more in London."

He stared at her, refusing to take the box.

"Nathaniel," she said sternly, sitting down beside him again. "While I appreciate you wanting to do things on your own, I am your mother, and I will always worry about you. If I can't take care of you myself, I will at least sleep better knowing you have more than enough to make do. Now, please, take it." She placed the box on his lap with an air of finality.

Despite wanting to maintain his stance, he knew she wouldn't budge. His resolve crumbled. It was foolish, he thought, to be upset when she was only acting out of love for him. So instead, he gave her a hug.

"Thank you."

"Of course, my darling boy," she said, holding him tightly. When they parted, they both had tears in their eyes. She placed a bare hand on his cheek, "You'll be all right, Nathaniel. You'll be happier than you ever dreamed possible. I know you will."

35

Nathan returned to his room and packed his mother's jewelry box into his trunk. Then, he grabbed the biscuit tin and set out to find Daniel. As he walked through the house, it occurred to him that in a few days' time, this place would be filled with people—family, friends, caterers, and more—all for Daniel and Sarah's celebration of love. He wondered if anyone would notice he was missing.

In the entrance hall, he crossed paths with Sarah. "I'm looking for Daniel," he said. "I need to give him something. Have you seen him?"

"Yes," she gestured behind her, "he's in the library."

He thanked her, but before he could leave, she put out a hand to stop him.

"Wait," she said, looking shamefaced. "I wanted to apologize, for before. You had every right to want to protect your brother. I'm sure I would've done the same thing for Andrew."

"Thank you for saying that," Nathan said and meant it sincerely. "Have you told Daniel yet?"

A small, pleased smile played on her lips. "I did, yes. Last night. It went better than I could've imagined. I can hardly believe I was so worried to tell him. He is such a kind-hearted man. In fact, we ordered a telegram to be sent to London this morning inviting Andrew to the wedding."

He beamed. "Sarah, that's wonderful!"

"We haven't told your parents yet, but Daniel assured me it wouldn't be an issue. He said he would talk to them himself."

"I'm glad to hear it. I only wish I could attend myself, but…"

"I thought you might be leaving," she said without surprise. "After this morning, I can see how much you care for Peter."

"Is that all right?" He asked tentatively. He didn't suppose that it mattered much what her opinions were—he would still be spending his life with Peter regardless—but he didn't want any lingering resentments between them.

"Nathan, are you asking me for my blessing?" she smiled wryly. "I daresay you don't need it. But if it means that much, you may have it. Truth be told, I'm glad Peter has someone like you. You have a good heart like Daniel." A pang of guilt flashed across her face then, and she shook her head remorsefully. "I truly am sorry about before. I said horrible things to you and made odious threats. I want you to know, for whatever it may be worth, that I would've never told your family about your predilections. I understand what kind of threat that would pose. In fact, I think Andrew is like you in that way. Though, I'm not sure he's realized that about himself yet."

"Is that so? Well, he will figure it out in his own time. I'll admit, I didn't know myself until very recently."

"You know, it's curious. I never saw it in Peter before, but after having met you, I can see it perfectly now. I do hope you are both happy together."

"Thank you, Sarah." He gave her a kiss on the cheek. "I hope the same for you and Daniel. Speaking of, I need to give him an early wedding gift before I go. If you'll excuse me."

"Of course." She stepped out of his way and watched him go. Before he was gone, she called out, "And do keep in touch!"

"I certainly will," he called back.

—

In the library, Nathan found Daniel sitting in an armchair reading a book. Upon seeing Nathan, he stood.

"How is your friend?"

"He's on his way home," Nathan told him. "I wanted to give you something. An early wedding gift. And an apology for not being able to attend. I wish I could, but Peter needs me."

Daniel stared at him for a long time, reading his face carefully, before finally nodding. "I wish you could be there, too, but I understand. You must go where you're needed."

"Thank you." He stepped forward and held out the biscuit tin to Daniel. "I wanted you to have this."

Daniel's eyes widened in astonishment. "Bless my soul," he said in a hushed voice, taking it in his hands with delicate reverence. "Wherever did you get this?"

"In the greenhouse. After all these years, it was still buried in one of the flowerbeds. Peter and I found it together."

Daniel carefully opened the lid and laughed to himself at the sight of their long-lost childhood treasures. "I can't believe I'd nearly forgotten about this. It's unearthing so many memories all at once." He grinned at Nathan. "Do you remember how angry Mother would get at us for digging up Mr. Millican's flowers?"

"Of course. Those were the times when I realized Mother could be scarier than Father."

They both laughed, and then Daniel smiled ruefully. "I wish I could've been here for the funeral. I'll truly miss the old man." He gently closed the lid of the tin. "Thank you for this. It is a wonderful gift."

"It is my hope that you share it with your children someday."

Daniel smiled and pulled Nathan into a hug. When he stepped away, he said, "Before you leave, I want to tell you something. Sarah and I had a lengthy conversation yesterday in which she told me something rather incredible. She has a younger brother! His name is Andrew. Can you believe it?"

Nathan tried to look as surprised as he could. "Does she really? Why didn't she mention him sooner?"

"I asked her the same thing, and she told me that in the beginning she worried that I wouldn't want the financial burden of supporting him—he suffered a rather terrible injury as a child, you see. And for all this time, she let this worry stop her. But then, she said that touring the gardens with you inspired her to finally tell me, because she saw, just by talking with you, how much love we have for each other as brothers. After that, she knew in her heart that she had nothing to fear by telling me."

"Daniel, that's wonderful," Nathan smiled warmly. "I, for one, will welcome Andrew into our family with open arms."

"As will I," he said. "I haven't yet told Mother and Father, but I'm not worried. With all due respect, their opinions don't matter as much as my own. Anyway, I wanted to express my gratitude. Without you, perhaps Sarah would've continued to keep Andrew a secret. So, thank you for possessing a heart so kind it inspires others."

Nathan swallowed around the lump in his throat. "You and Sarah are going to be immensely happy."

Daniel smiled. "As I think you and Peter will be, also."

Jude stepped into the library then and knocked on the doorframe. "Terribly sorry to interrupt, sirs, but Master Nathan, I've come to tell you that your carriage has arrived, and your trunk has been stowed."

"Thank you, Mrs. Fairchild. I'll be only a moment." He turned back to his brother. "It's a few days early, but congratulations, Daniel. To you and Sarah both. I wish you a beautiful honeymoon."

Daniel clapped a hand on his shoulder. "Do keep in touch."

Nathan smiled. "I certainly will."

36

"Are you certain you have everything you need?" Jude walked hurriedly beside Nathan to the manor entrance. The sound of heavy rain droned loudly outside. Thunder rumbled nearby.

"Yes, I believe so. Frankly, there isn't much I couldn't live without."

The sound of the thunder persisted as a long, low growl and grew louder. A sinking feeling crept into Nathan's chest. Perhaps, he thought optimistically, it wasn't what he feared it was. Perhaps it was, in fact, only the weather. But, as they rounded the corner into the entrance hall, they found that the door was already open, and a tall silhouette was standing in the threshold.

"*What the hell is this?*" Nathan's father growled. Jude stopped in her tracks. The rumbling sound filled the house. "I come back to my own home and there's another bloody carriage blocking my way. And the damned footman tells me it's for *you.* That you're *leaving.*" William, standing outside under an umbrella, peered nervously at Nathan from behind Lord Hambleton.

Nathan stepped forward. "Yes, Father," he said calmly. "I am leaving." He could see his father more clearly now. His eyes were wide and full of rage. The corners of his mouth twitched, threatening to turn his face into a snarl.

"*Goddamn* you," he spat. "I've had enough. You've embarrassed me in front of friends with your incessant need for attention, you've shamed this family's name, you've talked back to me, *disrespected* me, and most recently, you've turned my own family against me. Now, you think you're just going to leave? *LIKE HELL YOU ARE!*"

He charged at Nathan and grabbed him by the shirt. Jude screamed. Nathan tried to pry his hands off of him, but his grip was too tight. His father jerked him to the left and rammed him into the wall, knocking the wind from his lungs. He then set his hands around Nathan's throat. Nathan stared wildly into his father's hate-filled eyes and thought back to last October. It was on that night he learned that the violence in his father's heart was at the helm of his ship and would guide him wherever it wished. What's more, it wouldn't rest unless it was stopped by someone else's hand.

All those months ago, when his father attacked him in London—even when Nathan felt his closest to insanity—he still found in himself the desire to live, the willingness to fight. Now, he had more than just the simplest of survival instincts motivating him. He wanted a life without fear or anxiety or self-loathing. He didn't want the expectations of his father and others to burden him any longer. He wanted a life of his own. A life with Peter.

"*Father!*" Daniel yelled, running into the hall.

His father turned away briefly, and Nathan drove his knee hard into his groin. He cried out in pain and stumbled backwards. His throat finally free, Nathan took heaving breaths and began backing away toward the front door.

Sarah and his mother ran into the hall then, too, wearing bewildered expressions.

"What on earth is going on?" his mother shouted.

His father was already standing—albeit slightly hunched forward—and making for Nathan again, but Daniel was on him quickly, grabbing his shoulders to hold him back. In protest, their father wheeled around and shoved him violently, sending him tumbling backwards to the floor. He landed hard. Sarah gasped and ran to him.

"*VICTOR!*"

At the sight of his father turning on Daniel, Nathan saw red. Without a second thought, he ran up behind him and jumped onto his back, taking him off guard and causing him to lose balance. His father staggered to the right for a few steps before crashing heavily to the ground. He had managed to put out a hand in an attempt to brace himself, but as a result his wrist took the brunt of the fall. He howled in pain beneath Nathan's weight, his red and angry face pressed against the carpet.

"Nathaniel!" his mother cried out in alarm.

But Nathan paid her no mind. He quickly situated himself atop his father's back, pinning him to the ground with his hands and knees. His father let out a frustrated yell and tried to shake him off, but one of his arms was trapped awkwardly beneath him and the other was too injured to use. He attempted to push himself upright, but the tiniest pressure on his wrist made him yelp and collapse back onto the floor.

Panting wildly, Nathan leaned in close to his father's ear and spoke in low tones. "I never could understand why you hated me. I lost sleep as a boy, wondering what I'd done wrong. But I've realized now that I was never the problem. You were." His father gritted his teeth and tried to wriggle free again, but Nathan put a hand on the back of his head and pushed his face forcefully down into the carpet. "You are a pathetic, empty man who lives off of the admiration and fear of others when you are deserving of neither. You've destroyed your own family, and you have no one but yourself to blame. You are *nothing*. And I'm no longer afraid of you. If you ever touch me again, I will end your life. That is a promise."

Nathan sat back and took a steadying breath to calm the righteous anger coursing through him. Daniel was sitting up now, Sarah at his side. Everyone stared at Nathan with uneasy wonder; no one dared to move or speak. He then leaned back down close to his father and noticed a small pool of blood around his nose.

"You'll stay right here until I leave," he told him and slowly rose to his feet. The thundering noise from before had quieted to a dull and hollow whisper.

Jude hurried to the door and sent William to open the carriage.

Nathan walked to the entrance without looking back to the others and stopped beside Jude. He gave her a lopsided smile and kissed her on her cheek. “I’ll write,” he said, then ran out into the pouring rain.

37

In the carriage, Nathan held the letter with Peter's address close to his chest. He had left the summer home in shambles, letting others deal with the aftermath, and he didn't feel the least bit guilty. All that mattered to him was that he was finally free of his father and on his way to see Peter.

Day was quickly becoming night when they arrived at the train station. The train Nathan needed had left an hour before, and there wouldn't be another until tomorrow. He wasn't disheartened, though. He'd waited his entire life for the freedom he now possessed; he could wait a bit longer to see Peter if he had to. Thankfully, the rain had stopped.

He bought his ticket for the first train in the morning and settled onto a bench near the platform with his trunk. Nathan stayed put even after the last passenger train of the day had departed. The platform was well lit, and station employees worked into the early hours, loading and unloading trains that moved consumer goods by night.

The watchman walked by at one point and asked him if he was all right. He told him he was—just eager to get home the following morning. He dozed off at one point but was woken abruptly by the quick passage of a courier train speeding by the platform.

Finally, dawn broke, and Nathan's train pulled into the station. With his envelope in hand, he settled into his seat, leaned his head back against the rest, and fell asleep almost instantly. The rhythmic chug of the train ushered him into a deep and dreamless slumber.

Hours later, someone shook him awake. An elderly woman in a dark blue dress.

"Young man, if this is the address you're going to," she tapped the envelope in his hand, "then you'll want to get off here."

"Oh," he said drowsily, unsure exactly where he was. Awareness came to him quickly. *Peter.* "Oh! Thank you, madam." He grabbed his trunk, stumbled onto the platform, and set out to the ticket booth to ask for directions.

—

Nathan stood in front of the house he hoped was Peter's. It was a comfortable looking cottage with a thatched roof, whitewashed walls, and a lush vegetable patch in the front. From where he stood, he could see a barn behind the home and large fields beyond it with tidy rows of crops spanning from one end to the other.

This was the right house. He felt certain of it. But still, he was unexpectedly nervous. What if Peter's mother didn't like him, he thought. Or what if Peter suddenly changed his mind about everything? These were unfounded worries, he knew, but still they made him uneasy.

He quieted his doubts and let his senses take in the day around him. The sky still possessed the soft, youthful glow of morning. Fluffy white clouds grazed lazily over the crop fields. Birdsong floated towards him from every direction. It was beautiful here, and he imagined spending countless mornings like this one with Peter. A calm smile spread across his lips. He pushed open the small wooden gate before him and followed the stone path forward.

At the cottage's door, he was greeted by the aroma of freshly brewed tea from within. He knocked and waited. At first, there was nothing, but then came a quiet voice from the other side.

"*Come in!*"

It sounded nothing like Peter's voice, but still Nathan cautiously pushed the door open and stepped in with his trunk. Inside, he saw a quaint, welcoming kitchen and comfortable living space—a modest dining table, a cabinet displaying plates and cups and serving dishes, a generous wash basin in the corner, and large pots and pans hanging from hooks near the range that was nestled into the wall. There were several arrangements of dried flowers hanging about, some on the walls, some on the windows.

Sitting in a rocking chair near one of the windows was an elderly woman with a long steel-grey braid of hair. In her lap, she was sewing mismatched scraps of fabric together into a vibrant, multicolored rag rug.

Upon seeing Nathan, she blinked in mild surprise and then smiled. She had Peter's eyes. "You must be the boy my Peter cares for so much. He hardly stops thinking about you."

He stepped forward and cleared his throat. "I'm Nathaniel Hambleton, madam. You must be Mrs. Violet Watts."

"That's right," said Mrs. Watts with a twinkle in her eye. "I'm very sorry, but Peter isn't here at the moment. He went to speak with the vicar regarding the funeral."

"I'm very sorry about your husband."

"Thank you, but it's quite all right. I've known for some time it was coming."

Nathan glanced around and noticed that the curtains weren't drawn, the mirror on the wall wasn't covered, and the clock on the mantle hadn't been stopped. "Forgive my asking, Mrs. Watts, but is there a wake?"

"If anyone asks, yes. People can be so serious about tradition, don't you think? Personally, I'm not superstitious about these things. I was with my husband when he died, and I know with certainty that he has passed peacefully on to the next life." She looked at him pointedly. "I believe you know exactly what I'm talking about."

He nodded his head shyly.

"I wanted to thank you, Nathaniel," she said, returning to her rug. "For delivering the message to Peter. I do hope it wasn't too frightening for you."

He stared at her in amazement. "You mean, *you* made me aware of your husband's passing when I was in the conservatory? Has… Has *everything* been you?"

She laughed warmly. "Heavens, no. Think about it, dear boy. You've been receiving messages since you were a child, haven't you? Long before you ever met Peter, and therefore, long before I knew of you. Messages come from many different places, most of them unknowable to us, but I take credit for the one you received yesterday. No others."

"But *how* did you do it?"

She gave him a sympathetic smile, "Have patience. You're still early in your journey." She looked out the window then and sighed. "I'm sure Peter told you my memory is failing me. Some days are better than others, but I know it will worsen. Regardless of that, I intend to teach you what I can. In time."

His eyes went wide. "Do you really mean it?" He was immensely excited at the prospect of having a mentor—to finally gain a deeper understanding into his gifts—but in light of Mrs. Watts's declining health, he felt it was only appropriate to temper his enthusiasm.

"Absolutely."

"Thank you, Mrs. Watts. That's very generous of you."

"Please, call me Violet. And Nathaniel, I should be thanking *you*. You've been a wonderful influence in my son's life. You mended his broken heart—gave him purpose and hope again. And, whether you realize it or not, you've also helped him with the passing of his father. I can see that his perspective on death has changed since I last saw him. It doesn't frighten him like it did. When I told him his father is at peace, he sincerely believed me. My hunch is that he's begun seeing the world through your eyes, and I'm incredibly grateful for it."

Tears blurred Nathan's vision. "I can't express how much that means to me, coming from you. Thank you, Violet."

"And to think you were worried I wouldn't like you," she winked, and he laughed. "My goodness! Where are my manners? Here you've been standing this entire time and I haven't so much as offered you a cup of tea. I'd just made a pot, in fact…" She angled her head to the window as if she heard something. "Actually, the tea can wait."

Just as Nathan looked to the door, it swung open, and Peter stepped in. They locked eyes. At first, Peter looked surprised to see him standing in his kitchen, but shortly after, his face lit up with a breathtaking smile.

"Hello, Peter—" Nathan started to say, but was quickly cut off by Peter's strong body colliding into his. They both laughed and wrapped their arms tightly around each other, burying their faces into the other's warmth.

"I'm so glad you're here," Peter said in a muffled voice, and placed a small, discreet kiss on Nathan's neck. He pulled away and pressed their foreheads together. "I'm not sure I could stand another day without you."

Nathan smiled. "Well, I'm not going anywhere. Peter, my darling, I'm yours."

He cupped Nathan's face in his hands and grinned. He looked as though he wanted to pull him into a kiss but then seemed suddenly aware of his surroundings. He looked at his mother and Nathan did, too.

Violet was focusing intently on her rag rug and said, "Peter, why don't you show Nathaniel to your room so he can unpack? I'm sure he'd like to get settled."

"Good idea." He turned to Nathan with a lopsided grin, "Let me show you to our room."

Epilogue

Dear Jude,

I'm sorry I haven't written sooner. Things have been rather busy since I've arrived here. There were animals to feed, crop fields to tend to, and before I knew it, it was time to harvest and sell. It's been hard work, but I'd be lying if I said I haven't loved every minute of it.

Peter and I have been immensely happy together, and in fact, thanks to a rather generous donation given to me by my mother before I left in July, we are beginning a new business venture. As I write this, there are two large greenhouses being built on the property. We've decided to follow our shared passion for botany and become professional gardeners. Already, we've managed to attract the attention of a nearby manor house and have been commissioned to design a garden on their estate in spring! While beginning any new enterprise can be daunting, I have a strong intuition that this is the path we are meant to follow.

In addition to the greenhouses, I've made another investment—a lovely cottage that's near to our own. You see, our gardening business will surely demand most of our time, and as such, we need a housekeeper to assist us with the day-to-day affairs of the home. Naturally, you are the first person Peter and I thought of. It would be a fully paid position, and the hours of employment would be much shorter than what you're accustomed to now in the summer home. What's more, we know that Peter's mother, Violet, would appreciate the company of another woman throughout the day, and I can confidently say you two will get on splendidly.

Please understand, this is merely an offer. There is no obligation to accept. However, if you are interested, simply let me know and the cottage I mentioned before is yours. And before you insist—No, I will not accept payment for it. Consider it a long overdue Thank-You for being my dearest friend.

Sincerely,

Nathan

(I nearly forgot—If you do accept our offer, could you please bring my violin with you? I seem to have left it behind. I last remember it being in the greenhouse. Thank you!)

———

Nathan awoke naturally as dawn crept through the window and slowly brightened the bedroom. He stretched his limbs and yawned.

Stirred by the movement, Peter shifted under the sheets and turned to face him. “Good morning, love,” he said with a sleepy grin.

“Good morning, darling.” Nathan propped himself on his elbow and leaned down to kiss him. He pulled away and stopped to admire Peter’s eyes. They were always bluest first thing in the morning. He gave him another kiss, a slower one this time, letting himself sink into the soft sanctuary of Peter’s lips.

Peter kissed back, sighing contentedly and draping an arm over his waist to pull him closer. Nathan rolled forward onto him, his bare body rubbing against Peter’s. They continued to kiss, becoming increasingly more passionate and awake, their bodies responding eagerly to the touch of the other’s.

Then, Peter pulled away and looked at him with a worried look. “What day is it today?”

Nathan knew where his thoughts were and smiled. “Don’t worry, my mother won’t be here until tomorrow.”

His mother had written the week prior, informing them that, as much as she adored living with her two grandchildren, she needed a week of peace and, as such, would be paying a visit. This would be the fourth trip she's made since Nathan started living here. The first time had been a few months after he initially arrived when she had separated from his father. Violet had still been alive then, and the two of them had gotten along wonderfully. In fact, when Violet did finally pass, it had been Nathan's mother's idea for them to plant violets in every garden they created in memoriam of her. It's been a tradition they've upheld ever since. Regardless of a client's criteria, they always include a small patch of violets somewhere in the garden.

Peter sighed in relief and kissed him again. "Good. You know I adore your mother, but she's very punctual. I'd rather not hurry this morning."

Nathan grinned mischievously, "Me neither."

"It'll be at least another hour before Jude is by for breakfast," Peter said, sliding a hand teasingly down his back.

Nathan ran his fingers over Peter's chest and placed a kiss on his jaw. "Then let's savor every minute."

Thank you for reading!

And a special thanks to...

Cami
Joe
Raegen
Raimy
Selina

...without whom, this book would not exist.

Printed in Great Britain
by Amazon

39176789R00121